Penguin Readers

Penguin Readers

SURROUNDED BY IDIOTS

THOMAS ERIKSON

LEVEL

7

RETOLD BY CATRIN MORRIS
SERIES EDITOR: SORREL PITTS

PENGUIN BOOKS

UK | USA | Canada | Ireland | Australia
India | New Zealand | South Africa

Penguin Books is part of the Penguin Random House group of companies
whose addresses can be found at global.penguinrandomhouse.com.
www.penguin.co.uk www.puffin.co.uk www.ladybird.co.uk

Surrounded by Idiots first published in Sweden as *Omgiven av idioter* by Hoi Förlag, 2014
First published in the United States by St Martin's Essentials, 2019
First published in the United Kingdom by Vermilion, 2019
English translation by Martin Pender and Rod Bradbury
This Penguin Readers edition published by Penguin Books Ltd, 2025
001

Original text written by Thomas Erikson
Text for Penguin Readers edition adapted by Catrin Morris
Original copyright © Thomas Erikson 2014, 2019
Published by arrangement with Macmillan Publishing Group LLC d/b/a
St. Martin's Publishing Group, NY, NY 10271, United States. All rights reserved
Text for Penguin Readers edition copyright © Penguin Books Ltd, 2025
Cover image copyright © Pete Garceau

The moral right of the original author has been asserted

Printed and bound in Great Britain by Clays Ltd, Elcograf S.p.A.

The authorized representative in the EEA is Penguin Random House Ireland,
Morrison Chambers, 32 Nassau Street, Dublin D02 YH68

A CIP catalogue record for this book is available from the British Library

ISBN: 978-0-241-70061-7

All correspondence to:
Penguin Books
Penguin Random House Children's
One Embassy Gardens, 8 Viaduct Gardens,
London SW11 7BW

Penguin Random House is committed to a
sustainable future for our business, our readers
and our planet. This book is made from Forest
Stewardship Council® certified paper.

Contents

Note about the book

Do you ever think you're the only one making any **sense***? Or have you tried to persuade someone of something, with no success? Do people who don't get to the point drive you mad? Or does the way your boss talks to you annoy you?

You're not alone. After a terrible meeting with a successful businessman, who really thought that he was "**surrounded** by **idiots**", **communication** expert and author Thomas Erikson started a career studying how people behave and why we find it difficult to deal with some types of people.

Originally published in Swedish in 2014 as *Omgiven av Idioter*, *Surrounded by Idiots* is an international success, selling over 5 million copies in close to 60 languages.

It offers a simple yet **creative** way for **assessing** the personalities of people we **communicate** with—in and out of the office—based on four personality types (Red, Yellow, Green, and Blue). It also provides an understanding of how we can change the way we speak and share information.

Definitions of words in **bold can be found in the glossary on pages 136–143.

Before-reading questions

1 Who do you think the idiots in the title of the book *Surrounded by Idiots* could be? Do you ever feel that you are surrounded by idiots?

2 Look at this list of people's characteristics and how they behave. Put them in the correct columns for you.

amusing   calm   careful   able to concentrate
confident   creative   direct   dislike details
disorganized   don't like arguments
don't listen to others   don't mind arguments
don't worry   friendly   hard-working   indirect
interested in others   interested in themselves
kind   lazy   like details   like talking
listen to others   organized   prefer to be alone
prefer to be with others   quick   reserved
see things negatively   see things positively
selfish   serious   slow   shy
unable to concentrate   worry a lot

Things you like about yourself	Things you don't like about yourself	Things you like in others	Things you don't like in others

3 How do you talk to people who behave differently from you when you are working or studying?

4 Do you behave differently when you are with your friends and family from the way you behave at work or study? If so, how and why?

5 Do you think it's a good thing to have different types of people working together? If so, why?

The man who was surrounded by idiots

I was in high school when I first noticed that I had a better relationship with certain people than others. With some friends, we always found the right words, there were never any **conflicts**, and we liked one another. With others, however, everything went wrong, and I couldn't understand why.

I began to test people. I tried to say the same things in similar situations just to see what reaction I got. Sometimes we had interesting discussions. On other occasions, nothing happened at all. People just stared at me as if I were from another planet.

I just thought that there was something wrong with the people who didn't understand me. As I was the same all the time, what other reason could there be? I began to avoid these strange, difficult people because I didn't understand them.

Life went on with work, family, and career, and I continued to put people into two groups—good and sensible people, and all the rest.

When I was 25 years old, I was given the **task** of interviewing a man in his sixties called Sture. He had started his own business and built it up for many years. One of the first things he said to me was that he was **surrounded** by **idiots** in his company. He wasn't joking and he went on to explain why they were all idiots.

The more I listened to him, the more I realized that there was something very odd about this story. He had no problem in calling anyone an idiot in front of the whole company. This meant that his **employees** avoided him.

When you're young, you're full of great ideas, so I asked, "Who hired all these idiots?" Sture understood that I was actually asking, "Who's the real idiot here?" and threw me out.

It got me thinking. Here was a good businessman, who didn't understand the most important and **complex** part of an organization—the employees. Anyone he couldn't understand was an idiot. Since I was from outside of the company, I saw his thinking was wrong. Sture always compared people to himself. So anyone who wasn't like him was simply an idiot.

Although I never called people idiots, I didn't want to go through life thinking that I was surrounded by people who were impossible to work with. I didn't want to be like Sture. After a terrible meeting with him and some of his unfortunate **colleagues**, all of whom were angry, I decided to learn probably the most important lesson of all—how people **function**.

I began to study how to understand the people who seem so difficult at first. Why are some people silent? Why do others never stop talking? Why do some always tell the truth, while others never do? Why do some of my colleagues always arrive on time, while others rarely manage to? Why do I like some people more than others? Along the way, I've learned some incredible things that have changed me as a person, a friend, a colleague, a son, a husband, and the father of my children.

This book is about perhaps the world's most widely used

method to describe the differences in human **communication**, which is called the DISC—the **Dominance**, **Inducement**, **Submission**, and **Compliance** Ability—**system**. These words are the main **behavior** types, which describe how people see themselves in relationship to their environment. Each of these behaviors is linked to a color—Red, Yellow, Green, and Blue.

I have used different **forms** of this tool for over twenty years with excellent results.

There are, of course, different ways to become good at dealing with different types of people. The most **common** method is by researching and learning the **theory**, but this won't make you a world-class **communicator**.

It's only when you begin using this knowledge that you can develop real and functioning abilities. I no longer judge people just because they're not like me. I'm more patient, and I generally avoid conflicts and don't lie.

I have to thank Sture for making me interested in this subject. Without him, this book would probably never have been written.

One thing to note: To make this book easier to read, I have chosen to use "him" and "he" to talk about people in general. I know that you have enough imagination to read "her" or "she" where you need to.

Communication depends on the listener
All of us need to develop a **flexible** way of **communicating**, by **adapting** to people who are different from us. It doesn't matter what kind of behavior you have, or the method you

choose to communicate with, most people around you function differently from you. A good communicator is flexible and able to understand what other people need. If you know and understand how another person behaves and their method of communication, you'll better guess how they might react to different situations. This will also greatly increase your ability to get through to the person.

No system is perfect

This book won't give you a complete picture of how we, as people, communicate with each other. We could try to include details like: **body language**, differences between male and female speech, cultural differences, and all the other ways to explain differences in communication. But the number of signs we give those around us all the time just wouldn't fit into any book.

According to the *American Journal of Business Education* (July/August 2013), more than 50 million **assessments** have been made using the DISC tool. And yet, even with all this information, communication remains a mystery. We can't include everything. However, we can avoid the most obvious mistakes by understanding the basics of human communication.

It's been going on for a while

Different behavior patterns are what give energy to our lives. These include not just a person's actions, but the **attitudes** and beliefs that decide how a person acts. We can recognize ourselves in certain behavior patterns, but we neither recognize nor understand other types of behavior. We also act differently depending on the situation, making those around us happy or annoyed. However, while a person's actions can be right or wrong, there's really no pattern of behavior that is right or wrong. It doesn't matter how you choose to behave or how you're **perceived**. All behavior is fine, within reasonable limits, of course.

In a perfect world, it would be easy just to say, "I'm a particular kind of person, and it's OK because I read it in a book. That's just how I am, and this is how I act." Wouldn't it be great to always be able to act and behave exactly as you feel at the time? There are in fact two situations when you can do this: alone in a room, when it doesn't matter how you speak or what you do; or when all the other people in the room are exactly like you. In any other situation, it might be a good idea to understand how you're perceived and to learn how other people function.

Every kind of behavior is normal

Normal behavior . . .

- can usually be **predicted**
- is part of a pattern
- is changeable
- can be **observed**
- is understandable
- is **unique** to each person
- can be excused.

Why are we the way we are?

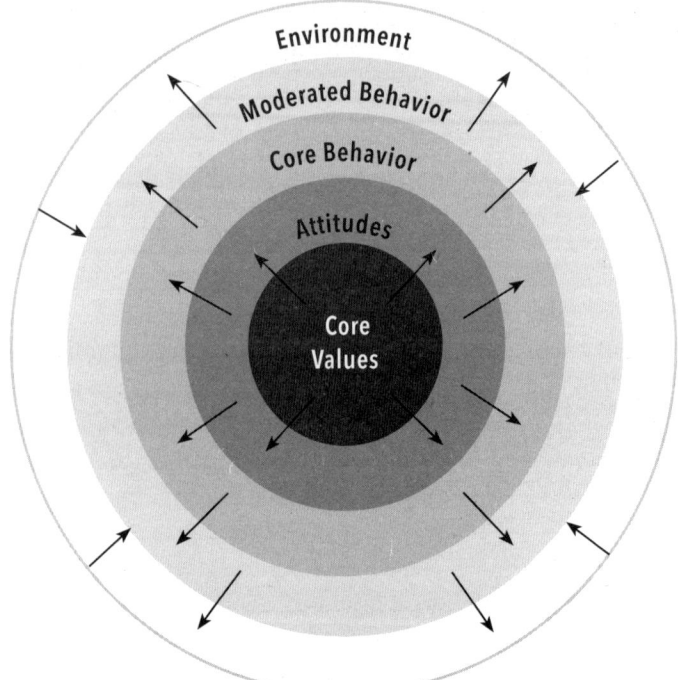

Where our behavior comes from

Where does our behavior come from? Why are people so different? It's a combination of **inheritance** and environment. Even before we're born, the qualities and personalities that we've **inherited** from our parents and our grandparents affect our future behavior. Scientists agree about this, although they're not sure exactly how it works. Once born, children learn and develop in many ways, but mostly by copying what they see around them, and especially their parent of the same sex.

Children learn **core** values at home or in school. My core values were "study and do well in school" or "fighting is wrong." Another important core value is that people are of equal worth. Attitudes are things I have **formed** opinions about based on my own experiences. Core values and attitudes together lead to core behavior, the real person you want to be, free of the **influence** of any outside **factors**, if that is ever really possible. But people around you most often see your moderated behavior—how you choose to act in a particular situation. Which means:

BEHAVIOR = f (P x Sf)

Behavior is a **function** of *Personality* (P) and ***Surrounding factors (Sf).***

Behavior is what we can observe.

Personality is what we try to work out.

Surrounding factors are things that we have an influence on.

Conclusion: We continually affect one another in some form or other. The trick is to try to work out what's there behind the behavior. And this book is all about behavior.

An introduction to the system

As you can see below, there are four main behavior types, each of which has its own color. This book is about how you can recognize them. Quite soon, as you start reading about the different colors, you'll think of particular people. Sometimes, maybe, even yourself.

Task-focused
and Issue-focused

Introvert
Passive
Reserved

Extrovert
Active
Implementer

Relationship-focused

How the system works

COMPLIANT (Blue)	**DOMINANT** (Red)
• Slow reaction	• Quick reaction
• Most effort to organize	• Most effort to control
• Least interest in relationships	• Least interest for caution in relationships
• **Focus** on the past	• Focus on the present
• Acts with caution	• Direct action
• Tries to avoid involvement	• Tries to avoid involvement
STABLE (Green)	**INSPIRING** (Yellow)
• Calm reaction	• Very quick reaction
• Most effort for connection	• Most effort to involve
• Least interest in change	• Least interest in **routine**
• Focus on the present	• Focus on the future
• Acts to support other people	• **Impulsive** action
• Tries to reject conflict	• Tries to avoid being alone

The **characteristics** of each behavior type

About 80 per cent of people have a combination of two colors that **dominate** their behavior. About 5 per cent have only one color that dominates behavior. The others are dominated by three colors. This book focuses on the single colors because they're the key parts of a person's behavior. Totally Green behavior, or Green combined with one other color, is the most usual. The least usual is totally Red behavior, or Red combined with one other color.

Many people you meet possess qualities that you sometimes wish you had. Maybe you'd like to be more **decisive** like Reds, or maybe you wish it were easier for you to **interact** with strangers, like Yellows. Possibly, you wish that you didn't feel as much stress, like Greens, and perhaps you wish that you could be more organized, as Blues naturally are.

Of course, it works the other way as well. You're going to read things that will help you realize that you, too, tell others what to do, just like Reds. Or that you talk too much, something that Yellows do. It might be that you take things way too easy, not getting involved in anything—the Greens' weakness. Or you don't trust things and see danger everywhere, just like Blues. You can learn to recognize your own behavior and how to take action to avoid it.

CHAPTER ONE
Red behavior

How to recognize a Red

"We'll do it my way. Now!" You quickly notice a Red person because he makes no effort to hide who he is. A Red person is **energetic** and determined. They push themselves hard, and they almost never give up. They've a strong belief in their ability to achieve anything, as long as they work hard enough.

People who have lots of Red in their behavior are **task-focused extroverts**, who enjoy challenges. They make quick decisions and are often comfortable leading and taking **risks**. In fact, people often think of Reds as natural leaders, and it's not unusual for a **CEO** or a president to have lots of Red in his behavior.

To say that they always want to compete is probably not completely true, but if there's a chance to win something—why not?

You can also recognize Reds by other behavior. Who talks the loudest? Reds. Who gives all their energy when explaining something? Reds. Who's always the first to answer a question? Reds again. And who, during a pleasant dinner, has strong opinions to give on just about any topic? Reds!

Something is always happening in the lives of Red people. They can't sit still and are always on the move. Doing nothing is a waste of time. Life is short; better get going immediately. Do you recognize the type?

"Tell me what you really think."

Reds are direct. When asked a question, they say exactly what they think, without the need to make it sound nicer. When a thought comes into their heads, everyone knows about it immediately. They've opinions on most things, and they share them quickly and **efficiently**.

People often say that Reds are very honest because they aren't afraid to say what they really think. They don't understand why people get upset. They've only said things as they are.

If you need someone with extra energy, you may want to invite a Red into the team or project group. They keep going when others have given up—if they're determined to succeed, that is. If a task is important, a Red will go through fire and water to complete it. But if he feels it has no purpose, into the trash it goes.

"Can I win something? In that case, I'm in."

Reds like competing. They enjoy both the conflict in a competition, and the great feeling of winning. They even enjoy winning competitions that are only in their own heads. It could be passing someone who is walking slowly in the street, finding the best parking space, or dominating the family game of *Monopoly*—despite being the only adult competing against the children. For a Red, this is all natural because he sees himself as a winner.

Time is money

"Quick" is the same as "good" for Reds. If you're in a meeting and suddenly notice that someone is doing something totally different, it may well be a Red who has lost interest. His thoughts may already be on the next step in the **process** being discussed. Because Reds are quick thinkers, they move on before everyone else.

Few things annoy Reds more than people wasting time. If a meeting or a conversation goes on too long, he may interrupt and say something like, "We've already discussed this for twenty minutes. How hard can it be?"

If you think about it, they're often right. When other people may find it difficult to make a decision, Reds are prepared to make quick decisions to keep things moving. With a Red on the team, things won't be discussed endlessly. It's always better to do something rather than nothing.

Anything is possible. Or is it?

Reds think that if we don't push ourselves to the limit, we haven't tried hard enough. They love difficult tasks, and they're extremely ambitious. Reds ask more of themselves than any of the other colors would, and they're always prepared to work hard.

All Reds are ambitious, but this shouldn't be confused with a need for **power**. Fearless Reds have no problem taking positions of power, but they're not always looking for them. Although making decisions and avoiding having to wait for others can be useful, having a position of power is not important to them. This is because they don't usually care what others think of them.

"Let me tell you how things really are."
When a Red has an opinion about something, or if he wants the rest of us to agree with him, he does everything possible to persuade us. When Reds believe something, they let people know that this is the only truth there is. There are two ways to do this—my way and the wrong way.

"What's the point of following the crowd?"
Reds are original and strong-minded. They're decisive and interested in results. For Reds, it's not enough to do things like everyone else does. Reds aren't afraid to make difficult decisions while everyone else is still considering the risks. It's of little surprise that many new businesses are started by Reds.

"It wasn't better before."
A Red doesn't try to keep to his original point of view if he realizes that there's a better **solution**. He has no problem changing his opinion, so he doesn't reject other people's ideas if he has none himself. For a Red, it's worth looking into anything that can move things forward.

Sometimes, his decisions can come a bit too quickly, but this ability to change brings a lot of energy and **flexibility**. If nothing has happened in a while, he'll push harder. Some people may find this stressful, but when you ask a Red why he changed something, the answer could well be "Because I could."

There are negative sides to this. Reds change things because they get bored easily, but the people around them have no idea what will happen next. When Greens and Blues have just got used to things and finally understood what they have to do, a Red will have already worked out the next step.

Conclusions on Red behavior

So, do you know any Reds? If you want to get to know some famous Red people, consider Steve Jobs, Franklin Delano Roosevelt, Venus Williams, Barack Obama, or Margaret Thatcher.

CHAPTER TWO

Yellow behavior

How to recognize a Yellow

"That sounds fun! Let me do it!" **Optimistic** and cheerful, a Yellow person looks on the bright side of life. These are people who like to live, always finding ways to enjoy themselves.

Do you know anyone who sees the sun where others see dark clouds? Have you met anyone who can laugh even though he hasn't had any good news for months? Then you've met a Yellow. If you've ever been at a party and wondered why everyone is attracted to a person, in the center there's a Yellow making everyone laugh. Every event becomes a wonderful party to a Yellow. When something is no longer fun, they move to somewhere the mood is better.

A Yellow is the one who's talking all the time. He's the one who gives answers rather than asking questions. He often answers questions that no one has even asked, by telling a story that may or may not have anything to do with the issue. But it really doesn't matter because he'll put you in a good mood. His positive attitude also makes it impossible for you to feel upset for long.

I would even argue that Yellows are more popular than other colors. They amuse people and put them in a good mood, and fun things always happen around them. They know how to capture everyone's attention and how to keep it. They make us feel important. They're just nice to be around.

Like Reds, Yellows are ready to make quick decisions, but they can rarely explain their reasons. They're likely to say things like "It just felt right." Yellows often make decisions that are based on feelings, simply because they don't think at all.

"Your friends are my friends . . ."

Yellows focus on creating relationships. They love mixing with people and can be extremely good at persuading them. They're enthusiastic, excited, and happy to talk about their feelings, often with complete strangers. Yellows can talk to anyone. They're not at all shy, perceiving most people they meet as pleasant. They even see strangers positively—they're just friends they haven't met yet. Their **optimism** has no limits and is, of course, one of their strengths.

Just like Reds, Yellows have lots of energy. They find most things interesting. Everything new is enjoyable, and a lot of Yellow energy is spent finding new ways of doing things.

Who gets the most postcards? Yellows. Who has the most contacts in their cell phone? Yellows. Who has the most friends on Facebook? You're getting the idea—Yellows. They've friends everywhere, and they're excellent at keeping in touch with everyone. Yellows want to know what's going on. They want to be where it's all happening, and they'll make sure to be at every party.

"Isn't it amazing? I just love it!"

Yellow behavior is full of optimism and enthusiasm. Few things can keep their good mood away for long. Yellows concentrate on finding chances and solutions. Nothing is really a problem for them, with their positive view of life.

I don't know where Yellows get all their energy, but it's focused on having fun and bringing people together. Everyone must be involved, and a Yellow won't allow anyone to be unhappy.

The optimist all around

Since Yellows are so positive and cheerful, they spread joy and warmth to those around them. Their optimism breaks down all opposition. How could anyone not be **inspired** by a person who refuses to see half-empty glasses and always thinks positively?

"What happens if we turn everything around?"

You won't find anyone more **resourceful** than a Yellow. If there's anything Yellows are good at, it's seeing solutions where others do not. Yellows have the unique ability to turn things around. They move quickly, which means that it can be difficult to keep up. Sometimes they find it hard to explain their wild ideas.

Yellows are helped by the fact that they rarely have any limits. When a Yellow is feeling **creative**, he'll try to go beyond what's considered normal. Usually, of course, a business sets limits for its workers, but this doesn't matter to Yellows. In fact, they often don't seem to know that there are any limits.

If you need help with new suggestions or ideas, look for the most Yellow person you know. Do you need a new look at an old problem? Speak to a Yellow. You might not be able to use any ideas they have, but one thing can lead to another and, suddenly, you have something that works.

Selling water to a duck

Yellows can persuade people with all their energy and optimism. They lose themselves in chances and solutions that others just don't see. It's often said that there's a difference between **convincing** and persuading, and many Yellows often confuse these. They don't just try and convince you with what they say, but with their whole bodies.

They've a unique way of communicating, which **influences** their listeners. They immediately know what to do: be friendly and shake your hand; say things that make you feel important. Many politicians are good at this—think of Bill Clinton, for example.

"I know lots of people. All of them, in fact."

Yellows inspire those around them, and the best way to do this is through building relationships. A Yellow knows that relationships are by far the most important factor in business. If your customer doesn't feel positively about you, it will be difficult to make any progress.

Yellows know more people than everyone else and they like everyone. A Yellow doesn't need to know a person very well before calling him his friend. They consider anyone who doesn't actively dislike them a friend. Remember that when Reds ask *what* is going to be done, Yellows want to know immediately *who* will do it. This question is key for Yellows. If the team or group does not function smoothly, a Yellow will not feel well. He needs functioning relationships for him to perform at his best.

Conclusions on Yellow behavior

Have you ever met a real Yellow? Famous people who show clear yellow behavior include Oprah Winfrey, Robin Williams, Ellen DeGeneres, Pippin from *The Lord of the Rings*, and Han Solo from *Star Wars*.

CHAPTER THREE

Green behavior

How to recognize a Green

The Green person is the most common. The easiest way to explain a Green is to say that he's the average of all the other colors, but this isn't something negative. Reds are stressed by their need to perform. Yellows are creative fun-lovers. Blues are **perfectionists**. Calm and relaxed, Greens balance these other more **extreme** behaviors. Not everyone can or should be extreme, or we would never get anything done. If everyone were a leader, there would be no one left to be led. If everyone were an enthusiastic **performer**, there would be no one to amuse. If everyone were focused on details, there wouldn't be anything to keep in order.

Greens aren't as noticeable as others, and they often bring peace to a situation. Where Reds and Yellows start fast, Greens are much calmer. Where Blues get caught up in details, Greens try to feel their way to what is right.

If you have a Green friend, he'll never forget your birthday. He'll be happy when you succeed, and he won't try to take all the attention with his own stories. He won't try to do better than you and he won't ask too much of you. He'll never see you as competition, and he won't tell you what to do unless he has been told to.

You can't ignore the fact that Greens are more **passive** than others. They're not as determined as Reds, not as resourceful as

Yellows, and not as organized as Blues. This describes most people.

For this very reason, they're easy to deal with. They let you be yourself. They don't demand much, and they don't cause problems unless they need to. Green children are usually described as little angels: they eat, sleep, and do their homework when they're supposed to.

Greens won't offend people if they can avoid it. They won't react if the boss makes a strange decision. (At least not to his face.) They usually try to adapt, which makes them more balanced people. They're perfect at calming down confused Yellows, for example. And they're excellent at bringing warmth to Blues, who can sometimes be cold.

A Green is usually very understanding of other people's strange behavior. Is the picture becoming clearer?

Greens are the people you might not think about—most of us, that is.

Some basic facts

Green people are kind. You can expect them to help you when you need it. They'll always do everything within their power to save the relationship they have with you.

It's often said that Greens are the best listeners. A Green will always be more interested in you than in himself. If he were interested in himself, he would never show it. You often find Greens working in jobs where they help others, without thinking about getting anything themselves. They're also good team players, and they'll always take care of anybody who is sick or weak. They'll always help a friend in need, and you can call them at any time. They always offer a shoulder to cry on.

They're not good with change, but if you can explain the need for change and give them enough time, even a Green is ready to try new things. A Green will remind you that you always know what you have, but you never know what you might get.

The best friend in the world

Greens are naturally friendly people. You can trust them when they tell you that they really care about you. Just like Yellows, relationships are important to Greens, and their interest in others is real.

If you ask a group of people if anyone can help, and nobody offers, a Green will jump in and shout, "Choose me!" Why? Because he didn't want to leave you in difficulty.

A Green will even help people he doesn't really like much, just to avoid trouble. He thinks well of most people and is confident in others' abilities. Sometimes this ends badly, but normally that's the fault of the other person, not the Green himself. He's so kind that sometimes others can use this in a selfish way.

He does what he says he will

If a Green says that he'll do something, he'll do it, if he can. He may not be the quickest, but he won't want to disappoint you or cause you any trouble. For a Green, the team (company, group, football team, or family) come before himself. It's natural for him to look after everyone else.

Everyone works well with Greens. In some situations, it's simply because Greens don't like conflict. Mostly, however, it's because they want to make those around them happy. The desire to please others is like a driving force for Greens. It comes naturally and requires no effort. This generous nature helps lower the stress of those around them.

"We don't want any unpleasant surprises."
Some organizations need employees they can depend on: not creative and clever people, but people who understand the job and do it. So they employ Greens. They're **stable** and will do the job well. They don't have problems taking orders—as long as the orders are delivered in the right way. Greens enjoy **stability** and a certain **predictability** at work, at home, with the family, everywhere.

When there's trouble, we'll see all kinds of interesting behavior in a group. Reds, who never listen to the whole message, just rush off to do what they believe needs to be done. Unless, of course, they're busy shouting at the management because they don't agree with their decisions. Yellows start wild discussions and give everyone their opinion on what happened. Blues will sit at their desks and begin the paperwork, thinking of half a million questions that no one knows the answers to yet.

Greens? They'll just talk quietly to themselves. If the management has avoided putting them seriously at risk, they'll carry on without complaining. There's no point worrying about it. They might as well keep doing what they were before. They're great at keeping calm and carrying on.

You'll always know how a Green will respond to some questions because he doesn't change his opinion very often. This isn't the case with Yellows: they don't know how they're going to react to different situations. Exciting—sure, but it's very tiring for those around them. With Greens, however, you don't need to worry.

"Who? Me? I'm not important."

Team before myself is a basic truth for a Green, and it shouldn't be challenged too strongly. The working group, the team, the club, and the family—all these are important for a Green. He often ignores his own needs if the group gets what it needs.

You may think that groups are made of people, and if each person is happy, the group will be. This might happen, but then the **focus** is on each member, rather than the group. The way a Green sees it, if the group feels good, every member also feels good.

Here the Green's kindness becomes obvious—he always thinks of those around him. This is partly the reason why it's difficult to get a straight answer from a Green. He's always trying to please everyone else. Everyone else is more important than him. A Green never asks for anything.

"I know exactly what you mean."

They say Greens are **introverts**, so they don't talk for no reason. When you're quieter than those around you, it's natural that you listen. And Greens will listen. They're interested in you and your ideas. Unlike Reds, who only listen when there's something to be gained from it, or Yellows, who usually don't listen at all (although they say they do), Greens hear what you're saying. They've a good ear for human problems. They understand what you've told them. This doesn't mean that they agree with you—but they're good listeners.

One idea that people often have is that Reds, and Yellows in particular, must be good at selling. This is true for sure. But what about Greens? We always teach people to talk less and listen more when they're selling, which Greens already do quite naturally.

Conclusions on Green behavior

Do you have any Greens in your family? Highly likely. Gandhi, Michelle Obama, and Jimmy Carter are people with Green characteristics. And, yes, Jesus. There's a guy who knew how to help others.

CHAPTER FOUR
Blue behavior

How to recognize a Blue

The last of the four colors doesn't bring attention to himself, but he does keep an eye on what is happening. While a Green will just let things happen, a Blue has all the right answers. He quietly studies, arranges, **evaluates**, and **assesses**. You know you've met a Blue if you visit someone's home and everything is organized. Clear labels and names on things so that the children know exactly where to put them. Lists of healthy meals for the next six weeks on the fridge door. If you look at his tools, you'll find that nothing is out of place.

He's also a **pessimist**—sorry: a **realist**. He sees mistakes, and he sees risks. He's the sad one, who closes the circle of behavior. Blues are reserved, **compliant**, and focused on detail.

"Excuse me, but that's not quite accurate."

We all have a friend like that. Think about it: you're sitting in a restaurant with your friends. You're discussing cats, football, or space rockets. Maybe your Red friend says that the American football team the Patriots have been to the Super Bowl twelve times.

Your Blue friend coughs and in a gentle voice says that the Patriots have actually only been to the Super Bowl eleven times—with their first appearance after the 1985 season, and nine times since 2001.

This guy simply knows everything. He doesn't shout about it, but his way of presenting facts makes it difficult for you to question them.

That's the way it is with Blues. They know how things are before they open their mouths. They've searched online, read the book, and checked the dictionary—and after that, they report in full.

But an important thing to note: if nobody mentions it, it's unlikely that your Blue friend will say anything on the subject. He has no need to tell everyone about what he knows. Of course, a Blue doesn't know everything. But you can usually trust that what he says is correct.

"I was just doing my job."

How can a know-it-all be so **modest**? It's rare that a totally Blue person would feel the need to stand up and tell the world who the real expert is. It's usually enough for him that he knows best. There are negative sides to this **modesty**. A Blue can watch a group of people trying to work through a problem together, then come forward after two hours and casually point out the answer. For him, it was never a problem at all. But because Blues often miss the big picture, they don't always act immediately.

There's also no need to cheer, **applaud**, or call a Blue up on stage when he's done something amazing. He'll just nod and then return to his desk, where he'll continue working on the next project. He may wonder what the big deal was about—he was only doing his job.

"Excuse me, but where did you read that?"
A Blue can rarely get too many facts or have too many pages of small print to read. For a Blue, no detail is too small to be noticed, and nothing should be left out.

Tell a Blue that he can ignore the details of the new contract or not read the last thirty paragraphs—there's nothing important there. He'll just ignore what you said. He would rather stay up late checking all the facts than miss the smallest detail. A Blue might ask, "Is there any more that I need to read?"

Why do some people have to consider things for so long?
Blues are generally very careful. They often think about safety first. Where a Red or Yellow would take a wild chance, a Blue will wait and consider everything one more time to get a full picture of things before acting.

This can be seen in different ways. For Blues, the trip is more important than where you get to, exactly the opposite of a Red. Obviously, this amount of care can result in no decisions being made at all, but it also means that Blues rarely take any major risks, which means that life is **predictable**.

A Blue generally creates systems that manage risks. They set three alarm clocks. They leave two hours early when one would be enough. They check and recheck the children's backpacks before school in the morning, even though they packed them the night before and no one has touched them during the night.

The positive side of this is obvious. Blues won't be surprised by unexpected events in the same way others would be. And in the end, they actually save a lot of time.

"It doesn't matter if it's easier. It's still not right."

Things can't be allowed to go wrong. Quality is all that matters. When a Blue thinks that his work might become low quality, he stops. Everything must be checked. Why has the quality dropped?

Engineers often have Blue characteristics. Accurate, **systematic**, focused on facts, caring about quality. Toyota, the Japanese car maker, probably has a lot of Blue engineers, as they have to ask "why" five times to check quality and solve problems. This is a very Blue **approach**.

Let's say someone discovers oil on the factory floor. A Red might shout at the person closest to him and order him to clean the oil. A Yellow sees the oil and then forgets it but, two days later, is surprised when he falls over because of it. The Green also sees the oil and feels a little bit of guilt because it's a problem and everyone is ignoring it.

A Blue asks, "Why is there oil here?" "Because something is losing oil." This answer is not good enough for a Blue. "Why is something losing oil?" "Because it's poor quality." "Why do we have poor quality parts in our factory?" "Because we were told to save money. We bought cheap parts." "But who asked us to save money and lose quality?" This is the way he goes on.

In the end, the Blue solution might be to look at how things are bought by the company instead of just cleaning the oil on the floor.

Blues argue that if they're going to do something, they must do it correctly. Because Blues usually find it difficult to lie, they'll always point out the problem that they find—even if this makes them look bad.

"If the path is different to the map, there's something wrong with the path."

Logical thinking is important to a Blue. Forget about all the feelings (as much as possible) and use **logic**. Of course, Blues can't turn off their feelings completely—no one can—but they say that they use logical arguments when making decisions. But they can easily get upset when things don't go their way, which has nothing to do with logic and everything to do with feelings.

Few people can repeat the same task lots of times in exactly the same way that Blues can. They've a unique ability to follow instructions correctly without question, as long as they understand and agree with them from the start.

How do they do this without getting bored or careless? Well, it's logical. If a particular method works, why change it? While a Yellow or Red finds new ways of doing something, a Blue repeats the same thing time and time again.

Consider putting together a piece of furniture from IKEA. Reds, confident that they can easily do this, start putting things together without even looking to see what's in the box. Yellows think that it's going to be great fun to get the furniture in place. They put parts together without really thinking. A Green puts the enormous box against the wall and has a coffee break. There's no hurry. A Blue reads the instructions twice, examines everything, and checks that the different pieces of the cupboard match the pictures in the instructions. He cleans all the different parts before he starts. It may take a little extra time for a Blue to put together his cupboard, but it will stand forever.

"Details are everything."

How do you argue with the instructions? It's impossible to find arguments that a true Blue will accept. The great value of this approach is obvious. A Blue will never be fooled; he'll always get what he paid for. It gives him an inner peace because he knows he's checked everything very carefully.

Under normal conditions, Blues are very calm and balanced. Probably because they keep an eye on everything.

"Silence is golden."

Introvert. I could stop there. Many Blues don't say a single word they don't have to. Does that mean they've nothing to say? Don't they have opinions about things? Of course they do, but they're just very, very **introverted**.

Blues are calm, stable people who are quiet on the outside, but anything could be happening on the inside. "Introverted" doesn't mean silent; it means active in the inner world. But the effect is often quiet.

In general, listen carefully when Blues talk because they've usually thought through what they say.

So why are they so silent? Among other things, it's because they, unlike Yellows, don't feel the need to be heard. Sitting in a corner and not being seen or heard makes no difference to them. They're **observers**, and can find themselves at the edge of a group where they observe and record everything that is said.

If you have nothing to say—keep quiet.

Conclusions on Blue behavior

Have you identified some Blues in your life? Bill Gates and Albert Einstein both used their attention to detail to build their success. We also have Sandra Day O'Connor and Condoleezza Rice. And, of course, Mr. Spock from *Star Trek* is the perfect Blue—all logic and intelligence, even if he doesn't understand all the jokes.

CHAPTER FIVE
No one is perfect

The differences begin to become clear

You've seen the differences between the colors in the Introduction (page 9). Some people focus on issues, others on people. While two of them (Red and Yellow) are quick to act, the Greens and Blues are thoughtful. This often leads to everyday mistakes, both large and small.

All of us have sometimes just stood there, unable to understand something we've heard or seen someone do, as it's completely opposite to how we would have behaved. And so we believe that they're idiots. According to this logic, "I'm always right," which of course means that the other person, and their way of behaving, is wrong.

A wise person once said, "Just because you're right, I don't have to be wrong." We also pay special attention to the faults of others. Experts have argued that the things we find most shocking in the behavior of our children are the things we recognize in ourselves—but wish we didn't do. So who decides what kind of behavior is right and wrong?

Time to say something obvious

No one is perfect or without faults.

However, when we think someone is an idiot, is it because of their faults, or have we misunderstood them? A characteristic that may be useful in some situations is not in others. Remember that communication usually depends on the listener. Whatever people think of me, that is the way they see me, despite the fact I might mean something different. It's all about knowing yourself. Good qualities can become bad ones in the wrong situation—it doesn't matter what the quality is.

A reminder of how each color behaves

Reds are quick and more than happy to take control if needed. They make things happen. When they get going, they love to control and can be hopeless to deal with. They can step on people's toes.

Yellows can be amusing and creative, and lift the mood of anyone they're with. However, when they're given too much space, they'll use it all, and they won't allow anyone into a conversation.

Greens are easy to be with because they're pleasant and they care for others. But they can be weak and unclear. Anyone who never takes a position eventually becomes difficult to handle. You don't know what they really think, and the absence of a decision can kill the energy in other people.

Blues are calm and balanced, and think before they speak. Their ability to keep a cool head is a great quality. However, Blues' **critical thinking** can turn to not trusting and questioning those around them.

Each color evaluates themselves in different ways. Reds and Yellows build up their positive sides and believe that they've no negative qualities. Their success often comes from ignoring their faults and looking for chances and good news. This can be hard over time.

Greens and Blues usually think about their weak points and sometimes even ignore their strengths. When you say something positive to a Green or a Blue, they can just ignore it and change the subject to something that went seriously wrong. Obviously, this is not useful.

How Red people are perceived

If you ask other people about Reds, you might get a different picture from the one the Red gives of himself. Reds think that they're surrounded by more idiots than the rest of us do. People usually say what they really think of a Red when he's not in the room because they're afraid he might get angry. You've heard him say that he wants to hear the truth. "Say what you think!" But as soon as you do, you find yourself in the middle of a lively discussion with an angry Red. So what you're going to read now will be completely new for many Reds. Not many of us have ever been able to make these points to a Red before. It takes too much energy.

Some people say that Reds are angry and selfish. They're perceived as tough, impatient, **aggressive**, and controlling. Suddenly, the picture is not as positive. The leader has a negative side.

None of this would upset a Red because he's more focused on tasks than on people. Anyway, everyone else is wrong. But let's see what others have to say.

"Why does everything take so long? Can't you hurry a bit?"
Reds have no problem in finding quicker ways of doing things,

not always following the rules, as long as it gets things done. A Red is often so fast that if something goes wrong, he would still manage to redo the project. At the same time, no one else ever really knows what's going to happen.

"I'm Not Screaming! I'm Not Angry!"

Because Reds are so direct, many perceive them as aggressive. This **perception** can change, depending on who the listener is. For example, in Sweden it's not OK to behave in the kind of direct way that would be fine in Germany or France because of a slightly different approach to conflicts.

In many workplaces, people are encouraged to be direct and "have open communication." Does this mean we should all be honest with one another and just say whatever we think? For any organization to be **efficient**, you need open and direct communication about important things.

So who can communicate like this and not get upset? Reds, of course. For them, this isn't an issue. "Why are we even talking about communication? It's obvious that you say what you think!"

Reds like to argue even about small things. They'll shout and hit the table if it suits them.

What does the Red want to achieve with this kind of behavior? It's to do exactly what you asked. You wanted an honest opinion! "Say exactly what you think," you said. It's possible you even added, "I won't be angry/sad/disappointed." "Be prepared," says the Red, "because here it comes."

A Red has no problem with conflict. Reds don't try to create conflict, but a quick argument every now and then can be a good thing, don't you think? It's just another way to communicate.

The worst thing you can do if you get into a conflict with a Red is let him win. This can cause you serious problems.

"What are you doing over there? I can see what you're (not) doing!"

What's behind the need to control? It's a person's need to have power over a situation with other people or groups. Those who need to control often feel extremely unhappy about having to adapt to a group or a situation and will try to avoid this. A common behavior is to talk or interrupt all the time, or ignore others, to keep control of the conversation.

It's important for a Red to feel that he can influence what people do and how they intend to act. At the heart of this need for control is a belief that they know more than anyone else. And because a Red feels he knows best, he'll keep an eye on everyone around him to make sure that they all do the right thing. This way a Red gets everything done his way, but everyone else feels controlled.

Some people think it's good when someone else makes the decisions, but others just want to escape.

"I try to care about you, but it would help if you were a little more interesting."

Reds are not usually interested in people. There's nothing wrong with that, as long as the person you're communicating with has the same focus as you. But if a Red speaks to a people person, like a Yellow or a Green, he can be perceived as very cold or inhuman.

Remember that we're talking about understanding and perceptions here. The aim behind a particular behavior is one thing; how we perceive it is another. It's just that you have to know a person to understand this. So if a Red asks you how your family is doing, for example, it's enough to answer "Great."

"It takes strength to be alone, and I'm the strongest of you all."

If we look at how a Red communicates, we can understand why many perceive him as selfish:

- "I think we should accept this idea."
- "I want that project."
- "This is what I think about it."
- "I have a good idea."
- "Will we do this my way or the wrong way?"

Add a sharp eye and particular body language and you'll see someone who will take what he wants. He'll fight for his interests. He'll tell everyone that he's capable of doing anything. Some people, especially Greens, find this "I" form of speaking uncomfortable. (Yellows use it, too.)

But we've learned to take care of each other. We know that being alone is not the same thing as being strong, that we need others to survive. So we think it's selfish when Reds speak only about themselves. They're often willing to walk over someone else if they see a chance for themselves. They might not mean to, but the effect is the same.

Reds often come out the winners in discussions. They see this as a natural part of a conversation. They always know best and will say that everyone else is wrong. It suits their character to behave this way. The result is that they lose friends, people can dislike them, and they miss information because no one wants them in the group. Once they've noticed this, they may decide that the other people are idiots.

How Yellow people are perceived

Amusing, fun, and very positive. Again—this is their own opinion. If you ask other people about Yellows, you may get a different picture. It's especially fun to ask the Blues. They'll say that Yellows are selfish, empty, and too confident. Others will say that they talk too much and are bad listeners. Combine that with the opinion that they can't concentrate and are careless. Suddenly, the picture is not as positive.

When a Yellow hears this, one of two things happens. Either he feels upset and hurt, or he starts an argument. But, over time, a Yellow won't really mind these opinions very much. He's a bad listener, and he only remembers some things. He forgets the difficult things, and with his positive nature he finds it easy to say to himself that he doesn't have any faults.

Let's have a look at what Yellows find hard—even if they don't always know it.

"Hello, anyone there? Listen to what happened to me!"
Yellows are very good communicators. None of the other colors come close to Yellows in finding words and telling a story. Yellows

love speaking in front of others. But they often can't stop.

A Yellow behaves exactly like most people—he does what he's good at. And he's good at talking. There are lots of examples of Yellows who completely dominate a conversation and don't listen to other people. Yellows have no problems in giving opinions, views, and advice even if they know nothing about the subject.

People say that for Reds, thought and action are the same thing. For Yellows, thought and speech are. What Yellows share might not be well thought out, but it almost always sounds very good. If you don't know a Yellow well, you might take everything he says as true—a serious mistake.

Very often, a Yellow is fun and can inspire people with new ideas. But in a conversation with a Yellow, you need to get your opinion in when you can, or simply close the meeting.

"I know it looks untidy, but I know what I'm doing!"

A Yellow won't admit that he's careless, but he has no natural way to keep an eye on things. He finds working in an organized way boring. Yellows avoid fixed systems.

The solution is to keep everything in your head. But it's not possible to remember everything, so the Yellow forgets, and people think he's careless. Missed appointments, forgotten dates, and half-finished projects, all because once his mind has finished the task, he doesn't go back. He goes forward to the next project. To complete a project, you need to be exact about details. Yellows aren't interested in details.

Generally, Yellows are good at starting projects because they're resourceful and creative. But they're not good at finishing them because they can't concentrate. A Yellow thinks that his work is good enough and doesn't worry about small things.

"I can do lots of things at the same time!"

A Yellow is always ready for new experiences. But there are so many new things! For a Yellow, "new" is the same as "good," so it's best that something new happens often. Without this, a Yellow loses focus. He doesn't want to listen to the whole story and all the details that may be important. It's not interesting to him, and he'll stop concentrating.

In a meeting, he may start playing with his cell phone or his computer or chatting to the person beside him. Everyone gets annoyed, but if no one says anything he'll just continue. Here Yellows are like little children. They continue until someone becomes angry, and then, of course, they feel hurt.

Because Yellows often quickly get bored, they're not so good at everyday things. New project—great! Put together a new and energetic team full of interesting people! Get everything going and develop ideas? Already done that! Working like crazy in the beginning to really get things going? Yes. But then? Following up on what is actually happening or not happening in a project is extremely boring. That means looking back; that's dull, and it won't happen.

"Me! Me!! Me!!!"

Yellows aren't more selfish than others, but they always seem to be. Why? Mostly because they're always talking about themselves. And when other people are not interesting and exciting, a Yellow will interrupt and change the topic to something far more interesting—often himself.

"You never told me that. I would remember!"

A Yellow is terrible at listening. Many Yellows believe that they listen very well, but somewhere along the way to the brain, whatever they heard simply gets lost.

It's not about memory. A Yellow is often not interested in what others say because he knows he could say it better himself. He doesn't stay focused; he begins thinking about or doing other things. He doesn't want to listen—he wants to talk.

Many really successful people don't talk as much as they listen. It's a way of getting new knowledge. This is something Yellows need to understand better if they're not to be perceived as completely hopeless—or just not developing personally.

How Green people are perceived

So what do other colors think about Greens? They're often considered pleasant, friendly, and caring. But a person who, out of fear of conflict, says yes but means no—how do you handle him? How do you know what he really thinks?

Reds and Yellows in particular have problems with this habit of remaining silent rather than speaking out. Some Greens tell the truth behind people's backs, leading others to perceive them as dishonest, although their aim is only to avoid conflict.

In general, Greens always expect the worst and therefore stay quiet. They're also unable to change, which others perceive as being afraid, **stubborn**, and cold.

Stubbornness will never be a good quality

What do you do with a person who never changes his views? Not even when the facts show that it's time to take a different path?

The difference between Greens and Blues is that while a Blue wants more facts about an issue, Greens expect things to simply be forgotten. They've made a decision about something and won't change their minds. Why? Because they don't usually do that.

It may have taken you your whole life to come to an opinion about the dangerous fat in food, or about space travel. Suddenly, this guy comes along and says that you should change your current opinion. It's not going to happen. The Green is waiting for the right feeling to come over him before he makes any changes. If it doesn't, well . . . they're often rather patient.

If a Green trusts someone, their word becomes law. This makes it easy to trick them because they can believe everything. Certain people use this against them.

Sometimes not giving up becomes a strength, but when those around them perceive it as pure **stubbornness** it can create problems.

"Nothing is worth caring about."

Since Greens almost always allow others to make the first move, you get the feeling that a Green isn't interested. And often that's true. He's more passive than active.

If you stay at home, nothing can really go wrong. What Greens fail to see is that most other people want to do things, not stay on the sofa. Greens are happy doing nothing. Anything that upsets this becomes dangerous. The result? Even more **passivity**.

The bigger the plans, the less likely it is that a Green will agree. A Green doesn't want people to be too involved because it's a lot of effort. Instead, let's just sit here and do . . . nothing.

What's thought in secret is said in secret

Greens don't take a position on sensitive issues. They've just as many views and opinions as anyone else, but they don't like shouting about them because it can cause conflict.

Instead of saying, "That's impossible," they may say something like, "It appears that there are a few challenges." Both mean the same thing, but by using less direct language, you take fewer risks.

For a Green, it's better to be safe than sorry. By being unclear, he doesn't have to **risk** his good name or take responsibility. If he hasn't taken a position in support of something, he also hasn't taken any position against something.

Greens are not focused on tasks like Reds and Blues, so they don't speak about facts in the same way. They would rather speak about relationships and feelings, which makes it more difficult to be accurate.

"I'll just think about it for a while."

If you want to make changes in a group with lots of Greens, good luck. If it's a major change, you should consider whether it's really worth the effort. If it's urgent, you can forget the whole idea. This is what happens in the mind of a Green:

- I know what I have but not what I'll get.
- It was better before.

- I've never done this before.
- The grass is *not* always greener on the other side.

Not all changes are for the better, but let's be sensible! While it's not always wrong to say these things, it can be very dangerous when change is really needed.

"I'm upset, but please, don't say anything to anyone."

A Green's hatred of conflict also causes many other challenges. Nothing is more important to them than keeping a relationship together. The problem is that their method doesn't work.

A Green will do nothing and keep silent in public even if he disagrees with something. But he'll talk behind your back so that the stress of not speaking out is let out. In small groups of two or three people, they'll happily show their feelings. And they're good at it. As long as they think that you won't notice, they can talk about you in ways that you would never expect from a Green.

How Blue people are perceived

People even find faults in Blues. They're perceived as avoiding situations, defending themselves, perfectionist, reserved, particular, uncertain, careful, not independent, questioning, distrustful, boring, distant, and cold. The list is long.

Blues find it difficult to begin anything new because they want to prepare so well. Everything involves risks, and Blues are always thinking about the details. Never put too many Blues in the same group. They'll plan into the next century without doing anything.

Many Blues are perceived as big critics who don't trust

anything. They miss nothing, and they give their opinions clearly. They create quality work, but they bring down the mood of those around them. They consider themselves to be realists. In everyone else's eyes, they're pessimists.

"Ninety-five per cent right is actually one hundred per cent wrong."

All this looking at facts and focusing on details can go too far. The importance of being neat and tidy can come out in different ways: it can be a person who can't cope with papers that aren't perfectly placed on a desk, who rewrites an email about fifteen times to get it truly perfect, or who works for hours on a simple presentation, just giving it the final touches.

"I don't really know you, so keep your distance."

We've all walked up to a person and started a nice chat. After a while, you realize that you're the one doing all the talking. If you have Yellow in your behavior, you may notice that there are pauses in the conversation. You may notice that the other person doesn't want to continue.

Blues don't like speaking to strangers. You may have been working together for a long time, but they require a lot of personal space, both for body and mind. He needs to know a person extremely well before opening up. Not like a Red, who says whatever he feels; not like a Yellow, who reveals his darkest secrets because he thinks everyone is interested; or like a Green, who can be personal, if only in small groups and in a controlled environment.

A Blue doesn't need to chat. It can seem that he doesn't

care about other people because he doesn't spend time on relationships. Sure, he cares, but his needs are different. He likes being in his own company and with family.

For Yellows and Greens in particular, he seems cold and distant. They call their Blue friend boring. Blues can easily make us feel uncomfortable. "Why is he so cold? Doesn't he care about me at all?"

"Think about it—three times if possible."

Where does this need for control come from? Why can't Blues trust other people or accept the information they hear? If they check themselves, then all the risks will disappear. But the fact remains that they don't trust others. Everything has to be checked, and recorded correctly.

Remember, we're talking here about behavior as perceived by others. A Blue checks everything one extra time because it's possible to check everything one extra time.

"The only thing I can trust is myself and my own eyes."

It brings you down to Earth when you tell someone about a new idea, and the first thing the person does is question every single point. Of course, if everyone looks long enough, they'll find mistakes. Being right is not even enough. You have to prove yourself to a Blue. If he considers you an expert, he'll be better at listening to you. The road, however, can be difficult.

The only thing you can do is accept that for Blues, the need for proof is much higher. Facts always remain, as we know: if I've prepared well enough, I can prove that what I am saying is true. In time, they'll trust me.

CHAPTER SIX

Learning and body language

If we had endless time, there'd be no problem

Learning something new isn't easy. But it's difficult to think of any subject more important than people. It doesn't matter what job you have, where life may take you—you're going to meet other people.

Understanding people will always be an essential part in achieving your goals in life as smoothly as possible. The **figure** below explains how **theoretical** knowledge is turned into real ability. Reading a book like this is one thing. It's a great way to start your own learning, but it's only the first step.

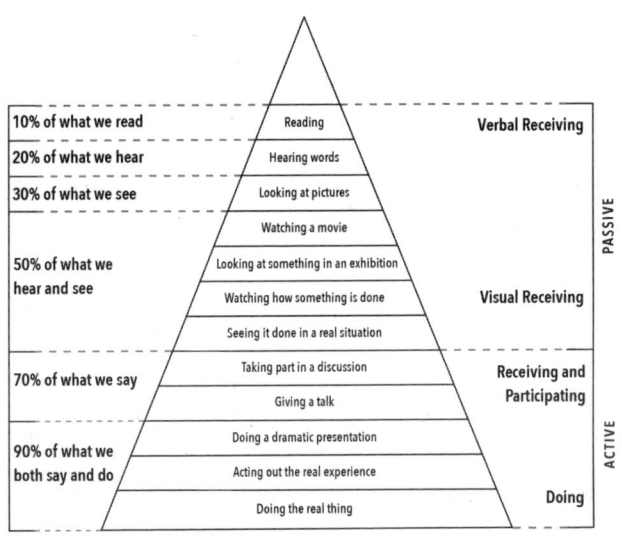

10% of what we read	Reading	Verbal Receiving
20% of what we hear	Hearing words	
30% of what we see	Looking at pictures	
50% of what we hear and see	Watching a movie	
	Looking at something in an exhibition	
	Watching how something is done	Visual Receiving
	Seeing it done in a real situation	
70% of what we say	Taking part in a discussion	Receiving and Participating
	Giving a talk	
90% of what we both say and do	Doing a dramatic presentation	
	Acting out the real experience	
	Doing the real thing	Doing

PASSIVE

ACTIVE

How we learn

A new approach

So much conflict could be avoided if we just understood why the people around us behave the way they do. We should be able to find other ways forward. Life consists of so much more than learning from your mistakes, some of which you can avoid altogether.

A language like any other language

The "language" this book discusses—DISC-language IPD (the Institute for Personal Development), which is the official name—works like any other language when it comes to learning. To study for your exams is one thing. To be able to really speak fluently is another. It's not enough to renew your knowledge once a year just before a trip to Spain. If you really want to speak Spanish, you need to practice with every Spanish speaker you meet, or you'll lose it.

Of course, after reading this book you can go out into the world and experiment with the people you meet. In the beginning, the challenge will be that you'll guess people's personalities incorrectly, and that may be embarrassing. But as you become more confident in the language of behavior, it will change how you interact with the people around you.

Body language

Different colors show different types of body language. As well as all the things you say and do, you show body language to the people around you. People use this to understand your mood. So let's take a closer look at how we move.

"Body language" is any **nonverbal** communication. Our body language also gives social and cultural information. The modern English language contains about 170,000 words, of which 5,000 are used regularly. Compare this to almost 700,000 signs that are used in body language. Our mood, situation, and whether we feel safe or unsafe can have an essential influence on our body language.

Posture—how we stand and walk

If you have a natural, relaxed, but not too relaxed posture, other people often think you're self-confident.

If you have a bent posture, it can be seen as giving up or feeling disappointed. If you're straight and a bit wooden, people can believe that this is a sign of **dominance** and that you demand respect from those around you. It could also mean that you were in the military.

Gaze—how we look at people

We use our eyes for many different things. If your eyes move around quickly, this suggests that you would rather be somewhere else. When people look at you directly, without closing their eyes, this creates a totally different effect. Everybody knows that if you can't look someone in the eye you're probably lying, so you should probably look for less obvious signs. (Someone who touches their neck a lot is often lying.) When something awful or unpleasant happens, many people put their hands up to their faces. And when you need to think, you often close your eyes.

Head and face

In conversation, we usually either nod or shake our heads, depending on whether we agree or not. When we listen carefully, we can move our heads to one side. If you drop your head or make lines on your forehead, you might be sad. When we're amazed at something, we often raise our **eyebrows**, while we turn up our noses at things we don't like. There are forty-three different muscles in your face, which you can combine in many ways.

Hands

When greeting a person, how do you shake his hand? A simple handshake can reveal a lot about a person. Weak handshakes often show **submissive** behavior, so it might be a good idea to press a little harder. If a handshake is firm, it probably suggests that a person doesn't give up. Anyone who presses too hard is probably submissive, but doesn't really want to be.

Clenched fists, like you're about to fight, rarely mean good news, and are usually aggressive.

Some nervous people remove objects like hairs from their clothes, as they would rather focus their attention on less important things.

Holding your hands together behind your back often means power and a feeling of safety.

A better way to know that someone is lying is if he puts his hand on his chest—particularly his right hand over his heart—and says crossly, "Would I lie? How can you say that about me?" This immediately catches people's attention because it's so extreme.

Personal space

It's very important that people have their own personal space, as everyone needs an area that is his own. This can be the distance you keep from people when you're speaking to them. The personal area, when two people who know each other are communicating, is generally a few feet. The social area, the space between strangers who are communicating, is three to ten feet. But this can depend on the culture of the speakers. In Northern Europe, for example, the personal area is definitely larger than in Southern Europe.

So what do we do about all this?

It's obvious that some "well-known" facts about body language don't apply to every person. Someone who is busily picking hair from his jacket might be bored, or he might just be nervous. Another example is how people deal with uncertainty. A Green who is unsure **leans** backward. A Red who is unsure leans forward, as his way of dealing with this uncertainty is to try to dominate the conversation.

Red body language

Some simple basics to keep in mind about Reds. They:

- keep their distance from others
- have **powerful** handshakes
- lean forward **aggressively**
- use direct eye contact
- use controlling signs.

Reds often have a recognizable body language from a distance.

You'll see a person who is walking quickly, ignoring the people in his way. With his eyes fixed on a point in front of him, the Red's steps are determined and powerful. He expects the rest of us to get out of his way.

The first time you meet a Red, he usually keeps a certain distance. His handshake won't be friendly, but it will be powerful. The Red—man or woman—will hold a little bit harder, to show who's the boss.

Forget big smiles. His face can be serious, particularly if it's a business meeting. But even in social settings, Reds are reserved. A Red won't give you a big hug.

When things start getting difficult—which usually happens rather quickly with Reds—eye contact will be very direct. When it comes to the language of power, they don't use many signs, but those they do use can be controlling and aggressive. Reds point at people and don't worry that this could be rude. It's also common that Reds use their whole hand stretched out to point toward you. Ask someone to point at you that way, and then think about how it feels.

You can also clearly see that Reds are ready to interrupt. They breathe continuously, hoping to find pauses in the conversation. If they have to wait too long to speak, they'll throw themselves into the conversation with a loud voice and simply take over.

Voice

A Red's voice is strong. They think nothing of raising their voices to make themselves heard. Reds can be nervous and worried about things, but usually you won't hear this in their voices.

This is one of their secrets. It doesn't matter what's happening inside, Reds will sound convincing. If we don't listen, they'll repeat it, but louder. In the end, they always get through to us.

Speed in speech and action

As we know, Reds are always in a hurry. Normally, this is true of speech and actions. Everything happens very quickly. Because speed means success for Reds, they won't stop unless they have to.

Yellow body language

Some simple basics to keep in mind about Yellows. They:

- touch people
- are relaxed and funny
- show friendly eye contact
- use large signs
- often come close.

A Yellow's body language is often very open and inviting. Smiles appear all the time, even when there's not much to smile about. They joke a lot and can be very relaxed. When visiting a neighbor he doesn't know that well, a Yellow may just stretch out on the sofa. When a Yellow feels at home in any situation, you can see it. He's like an open book.

The similarity with Red behavior is mostly in speed. Yellows move quickly and show strong self-confidence.

While some colors don't like having people sit too close to them, Yellows will happily move up very close. Yellows can suddenly start hugging everyone around them. Man or woman, it doesn't matter.

It's not **uncommon** for others to pull back when this happens, which Yellows don't understand. But it's not just that Yellows like hugging. It can also be any type of physical contact. A hand placed on an arm, a quick touch on the leg. What he perceives as something natural, others can perceive as an invitation, and it can end badly.

In general, with Yellows there will be jokes and smiles. Eye contact is no problem; it's strong, cheerful, and friendly.

Voice

A Yellow's voice shows strong involvement from start to finish. Laughter, fun, power. Enthusiasm. Joy. Energy.

Yellows are either with you 100 per cent or not at all. This can be heard in the voice. It goes up and down; it changes speed, strength, and power. Yellows' way of speaking is often like a song. It doesn't matter what emotion the Yellow feels, it will be noticeable in his voice.

Speed in speech and action

Yellows are not quite as fast as Reds, but their words fall out of their mouths, as they've so much to say.

Green body language

Some simple basics to keep in mind about Greens. They:
- are relaxed and come close
- act carefully
- tend to lean backward
- use very friendly eye contact
- prefer small signs.

Greens often—but not always—move slowly. When they're comfortable, their body language is relaxed, showing calm and confidence. No sudden movements of their heads or hands. Nice and easy.

Their signs are often softer and suit smaller groups. Greens don't feel comfortable in larger groups, so they become more closed and will appear reserved. Greens try to hide their true feelings, but their body language often gives them away. If they're out of balance or feel uncomfortable, you'll see it.

When sitting around a table, a Green will be leaning back, but they don't really have a problem getting close to people. Just like Yellows, they like to touch others, as long as they know the person they're touching. But don't touch a Green who hasn't given a clear sign that he knows you well enough. They can try to protect their personal space.

Unlike a Red, who you notice walking across a room, Greens don't want to be the center of attention.

Greens almost always have friendly faces. If he thinks that you're good friends, he can show it. If he feels that you've just met, you have to wait. Let Greens come to you. Don't force yourself on them. In time, when they trust you, they'll relax and become more natural.

Voice

A Green's voice will never be strong. You'll have to make a little bit more effort to understand Greens speaking in front of a larger group. Their voice will always be soft and warm, but not as varied as a Yellow.

Speed in speech and action

Generally, Greens speak more slowly than Reds and Yellows, but not quite as slow as Blues. Speed is not important. If it risks stopping the group working together, Greens will reduce the speed. The most important thing is always going to be how people feel.

Blue body language

Some simple basics to keep in mind about Blues. They:
- prefer to keep others at a distance
- either stand or sit
- often have closed body language
- use direct eye contact
- speak without signs.

The easiest way to describe a Blue's body language is to say that he has none. Neither his face nor his body reveals much.

Many Blues say **dramatic** things without changing their faces. This gives people the idea that Blues have no feelings, but that's not true. A Blue is an introvert, so most of his emotions simply occur inside him.

Just like Greens, Blues have no need to be the center of attention. The difference, however, is that while a Green wants to run away from large groups, a Blue remains standing.

Blues require a lot of personal space, and often feel more comfortable at a distance. Naturally, it depends on how well they know other people, but this area is much larger than it is for Yellows.

If others come too near, Blues' body language becomes closed.

Both arms and legs will be crossed.

Blues also move less than others and can stand still for a whole hour while giving a talk. When they sit down, they remain more or less in the same position all the time. So they won't use too many signs.

However, Blues normally look others straight in the eyes. They've no problem with eye contact, even if it makes others uncomfortable.

Voice

A Blue's voice is not weak, but reserved and quiet. It's common for them to sound very thoughtful.

Generally, there's little or no change in a Blue's voice. He sounds more or less the same all the time—not musical.

Speed in speech and action

Compared to others, they're slow. Speed is of no interest to them.

CHAPTER SEVEN

Adapting

What do you do about the differences between people?

It's natural for us to be who we are, to show our core behavior. But we can be flexible and **adaptable** in dealing with situations and responding to different types of people. This has a name— EI (emotional intelligence).

This kind of **adaptation** requires ability, training, and energy: it's not natural for us to adapt all the time. If we're uncertain as to what is "right" in a situation, we'll be frightened, unsure, and often stressed. As a result, we lose more energy and our core behavior can be seen clearly—often to the surprise of those around us, who are used to seeing us behave in a certain way.

In a perfect world

In the perfect world, everyone can be themselves and everything functions smoothly. Everyone agrees at all times and there are no conflicts. But it's not that simple. If you think that you can change everyone else, you'll be very disappointed. It would be surprising if you could change anyone at all.

It doesn't matter if you're Red, Yellow, Green, or Blue, or a combination of different colors—there will always be fewer of you than them. Most of the people you meet will be different from you. You can never be balanced enough to be all the types at the same time. So you have to adapt to the people you meet.

Good communication is about adapting to others.

Don't expect to get through to other people with a message you're trying to share. If you can accept that most of the people you meet won't believe what you say, then you don't have a problem.

In this world

We all adapt to one another all the time, even if we don't think we do. It's part of the social game that is always in progress. You can make adjustments from the beginning. But please note: no system is perfect. There are always exceptions.

There are two parts to adaptation for each color. The first part deals with what you need to do to interact with the other person and make him feel that you understand him. The second part deals with how you get people to take your side.

What a Red expects of you
"Do what I asked you, as quickly as possible!"

If you ask a Red, he'll agree that most people speak too slowly, have trouble coming to the point, and they don't work well. In a Red's world, everything simply takes too long.

Thought and action are one. It has to be done quickly. Reds dislike endless discussion.

Conclusion: If you want to adapt to a Red—hurry up! Speak and act quickly. Look at the clock often, like a Red. Finish a meeting in half the time if you can. Don't drive too slowly with a Red in the car.

"Do you want something? Speak up!"

As you now know, Reds get to the point, and they enjoy being with other people who tell them what they want—quickly. If you go around in circles, a Red will get tired. And he knows when you're just chatting.

Conclusion: If you want to have a Red's full attention, cut the chat. Be clear and direct, and start with the most essential point of your message. Don't say or write a single word you don't need. Make sure you've done your homework. He may have questions if he **senses** that you're uncertain.

"I don't care what you did on vacation."

Reds live for the here and now. They've a unique ability to focus on the present. They've no problem with **creativity** or new ideas, as long as it moves you forward. But conflict is never far off. The best method for a Red is to establish what the problem is and then just get to work.

Conclusion: Stay on task! Prepare very carefully before going into a meeting with a Red. If, in the middle of a discussion, another thought comes into your head, write it down and ask at the end of the meeting if it's OK to raise the issue. Or plan a new meeting.

Reds can become annoyed and aggressive when they notice that someone is trying to be friends with them. A Red isn't here to be your friend. He's here to do business. He might throw you out if he thinks you're just trying to win him over.

Conclusion: Reds are actually the easiest to sell to. All you need to do is present your suggestions, and then ask about a deal. Don't chat. When a Red trusts you, then he may start discussing cars, boats, or politics. Even then, don't be surprised if the meeting ends suddenly because he's tired of the conversation.

"Why am I wasting my time with you?"

A Red would also like you to be firm and direct. Although he likes making all the important decisions himself, he strongly dislikes dealing with uncertain people.

If you have an opinion, give it. Reds judge you on how determined you are. Listen to them, of course, but you must have an opinion of your own, or they'll think you're weak. That's not a quality that they like.

Conclusion: Deliver your opinion directly, even if a Red tries to change your mind **energetically**. The worst thing you can do is give up. A Red will lose respect for you.

The best thing you can do is place yourself in the center of the storm, telling him that he's wrong. When a Red discovers that you won't give up, he'll turn to your point of view.

"You can sleep when you're dead."

If you've a boss who's Red, he'll work hard, maybe harder than anyone else you've ever met. He'll do lots of different things at the same time, and he'll have complete control over everything. A Red can accept that everything won't be right the first time. But he'll demand that you work hard and will think a lot of you because of it.

Conclusion: Show that you work hard, without telling him

70

every detail. But report back regularly about what you've done and briefly present the result of your efforts.

Take the lead. Offer suggestions that the Red didn't ask for. As usual, get ready to fight, but he'll like your determination.

How to behave when you meet a Red

You don't have to completely adapt to how Reds want you to behave, but there are things you need to do to achieve the best results.

"Details . . . Boooooring . . ."

Essentially, Reds dislike details. They can be careless about small, boring things, which take time. For them, results are more important than the journey. Reds won't naturally stop to consider details or **analyze** their method.

Conclusion: If you want to help Reds do better work, try to show how useful it is to keep an eye on the details. Explain that the results will be better and **profits** larger. They might not want to follow your advice, but if you're good at arguing, they will. We know that Reds are good at pushing themselves, as long as they're moving forward.

Quick but often wrong

Everything in a Red's world is usually very urgent, and this leads to risks.

A Red needs someone who can make him pause and realize that not everyone understands the situation as quickly as he does. He'll never be able to do every part of a project on his own—

even if he believes he can. He needs to have his team with him.

Conclusion: Give examples of where time was lost by being too fast. Point out the risks involved in hurrying. Explain that others can't keep up, and point out that it would be great if everyone knew what the project was about. Don't give up. Say that not even he can manage everything himself. Make a Red wait for others. After this, show clearly what was gained from taking things a bit slower.

"Let's try some untested ideas and see what happens."

Should we really do that? Many Reds actively search for risks. In fact, what others might perceive as dangerous behavior, a Red wouldn't even think of as **risky**.

However, Reds do need someone to weigh the positives and the negatives, which are boring. Since information about risks often lies in the details, your approach should focus on them.

Conclusion: Since Reds prefer to focus on the present and the future, an honest discussion of experiences is needed. Prove things with facts, and demand that he checks before deciding to take on a new project.

"I'm not here to be your friend."

Reds may not understand that others are avoiding them because they don't like conflict. This means that Reds don't always receive important information.

Conclusion: Reds need to understand that the road to openness is to adapt to others. By realizing that no one can manage everything alone, they may pause and actually care about other people. Once a Red understands what all this chatting is about, the door is open. You may even learn something about him.

"How weak are you? Just deal with it!"

Reds get angry. They don't notice it happening themselves; screaming a little bit is just another way to communicate. When a Red behaves like this, you must tell him nicely that's not how it works.

Conclusion: You should deal with his behavior immediately. Just say loudly and clearly that you won't tolerate rudeness, nastiness, or bad temper. Tell him he must behave like an adult, and if he loses his temper, just leave the room.

Reds hate being told to be quiet more than anything else.

What a Yellow expects of you
"Isn't it nice being here all together?"

Yellows are not afraid of conflict. If something goes wrong, they can get annoyed, but they prefer a pleasant atmosphere. Yellows are at their best when everyone is friendly and the sun is shining.

However, a Yellow can be very sensitive to whether people are in a good mood or not. If there's **aggression** in the air, he won't be happy at all.

Conclusion: A Yellow functions best when he's happy, he's feeling creative, and he has positive energy. You should try to create a warm and friendly environment. Smile a lot, have fun, and laugh. If you do that, he'll feel better about you and listen to you more. A Yellow in a bad mood isn't much fun.

"I asked someone to do that—I can't remember who."

Keeping a Yellow's interest isn't easy. There are many things that a Yellow employee, customer, friend, or neighbor finds boring.

Don't give a Yellow lots of details. It just gets boring. Not only will he forget what you're talking about, but he'll just think that he doesn't need any of those details. His strength lies in other things. You can easily ask a Yellow to make a plan for the next ten years, but don't ask him to explain how to make it happen.

Conclusion: If you want to keep a Yellow's attention, take away as much detail as you possibly can. Always start with the big questions. It's just like with Reds, if not worse. Yellows don't care about how things work, only that they work.

Follow your feelings

A Yellow can ignore the actual facts so long as it feels right. He's not stupid. He understands that facts are important. He's just not interested.

Conclusion: Just accept that a Yellow wants to feel his way. He doesn't mind not being sure and isn't really afraid of risks. Adapt to it. You can communicate with him by showing him that you, too, follow your feelings.

"No one has done this before? Perfect!"

While a Red focuses on speed, a Yellow focuses on the latest and greatest. "New" means "good." All Yellows know that. Without creating and inventing new things, there would be no development, right?

Conclusion: Allow a Yellow to spend time on the latest thing. He'll love it. If you want to sell something to a Yellow, say things like "newly developed" and "never before used."

"You seem interesting. Do you want to know who I am?"
Yellows function best if they're in a crowd. Of course, Yellows don't like everyone they meet, but they'll give most people a chance.

You need to show a Yellow that you're just as open and friendly as he is. If you're too closed and private, he'll feel unwelcome. If you're Red or Blue, you need to think carefully about how to get this to work.

Conclusion: Become **approachable**. Show that you're available; smile a lot; be sure to have open body language. You should show interest in the Yellow as a person. It won't be difficult to find out things about him because he'll freely tell you.

How to behave when you meet a Yellow

To make progress with Yellows, you need to do more than just create a great environment. Once you're speaking their language, you need to do the following.

Learn to tell whether a Yellow is listening

Yellows are the worst listeners. Usually, they'll never admit it. Many Yellows actually see themselves as good listeners, but they don't want to listen. They want to talk. Yellows think that they can say everything better than anyone else. The problem is that they ignore what anyone else is saying.

Conclusion: When you're dealing with Yellows, you need to know what your message is and exactly what response you need from them. But be prepared to return to it if it's important because the Yellow didn't write anything down.

Learn how to respond to "No problem—that won't take long at all!"

Yellows are time **optimists**. Sure, your work can be done quickly, but rarely as quickly as a Yellow thinks. This is because he can't plan his life.

The problem is obvious. It's impossible to achieve everything a Yellow wants to do because he doesn't know how long anything takes. The other problem is that he won't start when he should.

Conclusion: Organize all appointments very carefully with Yellows, and check your watches.

It looks like a bomb went off in here

Untidy desks, rooms, and bags belong to Yellows. Meetings are moved or forgotten; things disappear; keys and even whole cars are lost. Many Yellows can't even plan their day. They can go to the supermarket five times and buy three things at a time because they didn't write it down. (Yet Yellows think they've the best memory in the world.)

Conclusion: If you really want to help a Yellow get organized, help him create lists. They need them, but be careful because they hate them.

The most important thing is to look good all the time

Just like Reds, Yellows like getting attention and throw themselves into the center of things faster than anyone else. Your Yellow friend is talking louder and faster than everyone else and lighting up a room with his behavior. No one else gets any space. It doesn't matter what you're talking about, a Yellow has a story about himself, or he'll invent one.

Their thoughts often begin with the word "I." "I want," "I think," "I can," "I know," "I will." They like other people, but they like themselves even more.

Conclusion: Yellows need to understand that there are other people in the room. You can never allow Yellows to dominate. They need to learn to let others enter the conversation. Yellows can be hurt by such **criticism**. You need to talk to a Yellow privately and in a positive way. But you may become enemies in the process.

All talk, but no walk

Yellows talk more than they work. They prefer talking rather than actually doing anything. Many people find it hard to do boring tasks, but Yellows find lots of creative excuses for avoiding them.

A Yellow spends more time talking about the future than getting there.

Conclusion: To help your Yellow friend, you need to push him gently, treating him like you would a child. Be kind but clear. Yellows hate feeling controlled, so you need to move carefully.

Take a moment to explain to a Yellow how everyone will love him even more.

Yellows don't take criticism well

It's obvious to everyone, even Yellows, that all of us make mistakes and no one is perfect. The problems come when we try to make a Yellow understand that he may need to improve. This creates a conflict, especially if the criticism is public.

Yellows don't deal well with criticism. They don't like it because it doesn't make them look good. Deep down, the Yellow knows that he has faults; he just won't consider talking about them.

Conclusion: If you wish to say something negative to a Yellow, create a friendly environment and carefully prepare what you want to say. Clearly repeat your message until he understands, and get real answers to your questions. Insist that he writes down what you have said and ask him to repeat it to you.

What a Green expects of you
Everything should feel good all the time

A Green worries about everything, so he hides. If you don't see something, it's not there. He wants stability and doesn't want to think about risk. And since he doesn't really want to get out into the world, it's easier to just stay at home, where it's nice and safe.

Conclusion: Accept that this person doesn't think like you do and is driven as much by fear as by anything else. Show that you're ready to listen to his worries. We all have things we worry about; a Green just has more of them.

Help your Green friend to face his fear of the unknown. Encourage him to be brave and move ahead.

Nothing happened. Twice

For a Green, nothing is too big to be ignored. Being active and determined—these things disturb their peace. Greens feel better when they don't have to be active. Peace and quiet make them feel safe and happy.

Conclusion: It's important to put yourself in other people's shoes, knowing how stressful it can be for them to do things all the time. The solution is to allow the Green his periods of peace, quiet, and inactivity. He needs to be allowed to do a reasonable amount of—nothing.

"I think I'll pass on that . . ."

Stability and predictability are valuable to a Green. It's good to know what's going to happen. We probably all feel a bit like that. For Greens, this need is very strong. When Reds ask what, Yellows wonder who. When Blues ask why, Greens want to know how.

A Green needs to know what the plan is. What needs to happen? When will things be taking place? What should he expect? But their need for predictability goes further than that. In our society today, the only thing that's permanent is change. This is extremely stressful for Greens.

Conclusion: Since a Green won't think of anything on his own, you need to help him plan. Maybe by explaining every step, you can stop him worrying. But make sure you share the plans with him, or there's a risk he'll run away.

How to behave when you meet a Green

OK, now you know how Greens like to be handled. The result will be a calm and excellent relationship, and you'll be good friends for many years. But you can't stop there because, unless you're a Green yourself, you'll want to actually do something every now and then. And you'll need to have some ideas about how to get him moving.

"Why does everything have to be so complex?"

Greens don't like conflict of any kind. They lock themselves in and become silent and passive if there's any sign of it.

Conclusion: Be careful how you present any opinions on a Green's behavior. Make sure the Green understands that you still like him, but that you believe that he and the group will function better if he changes certain things. Don't ask him what he can do about the behavior; just ask him to do certain things. It may be that he knows what to do, but, as usual, he won't lead the conversation—you'll need to do that.

"It was much better before."

Most people have Green as their **dominant** color, and this is the main reason we can't accept change with open arms. Fast change is the most difficult to accept. The faster it is, the worse it is. Yellows and Reds create change, while Greens and Blues, most of us, try to keep up. And the stress just increases.

Conclusion: If you want Greens to accept change, you'll have to be patient. Break down the process into small pieces and allow time to persuade, win over, and explain details.

The group must get the chance to feel its way to the only possible solution—change.

Someone needs to lead us

Greens don't have clear leadership qualities, particularly as being a leader is often about bringing in change. Luckily, this doesn't mean that there are no good Green bosses—there are many of them out there. However, they won't step forward in the same way as Reds and Yellows do. Often they don't want any responsibility because:

a) it can lead to conflict if someone doesn't agree with a decision, or

b) there may be lots of extra work, and that's never good.

And so they avoid it, for as long as possible.

Greens (and some other colors on occasion) can blame everything and everyone but themselves.

Given the passivity a Green person can show, we immediately end up with problems.

Conclusion: If you want to make progress with a large group of Greens, you have to take control. Asking a group of Greens to solve a task is pointless, unless you put them on track. But do it gently . . .

What a Blue expects of you
Think of everything from the beginning
A Blue prepares carefully. A Blue has gone through all the information, analyzed everything down to the smallest detail, and he'll be prepared to discuss anything on the topic. He'll have a plan B and a plan C.

He's thought of everything, so you should, too
Being Blue is a little like being in the military: no excuses are allowed. You should be prepared for everything. Don't say something like, "That's just the way it is." The next time you meet him, he'll have less confidence in you.

Conclusion: Make sure you can show that you've done your homework and are well prepared. Don't make a big deal out of knowing the answer. He expected it. And—most important—if you don't have the answer, just say so.

We're not here to be friends
Make sure to stay focused on the task. A Blue isn't interested in your personal tastes.

Conclusion: Keep to the task. Work with checklists where facts are noted. Don't ask personal questions. In time, he'll open himself up to you if he wants to. It's not that he doesn't like you; he just wants to work first. Accept this and it will go well.

Let's all stay in the real world
Blues use their critical minds to judge whether things are **realistic** or not. You may think they're **pessimistic** or don't

trust you. They believe they're realists. If a plan seems crazy, a Blue will never have any confidence in it. Don't try to promote wild ideas. What you say needs to be realistic.

Conclusion: Think through what you want to say, and what you want to persuade a Blue to believe. Put dreams to one side. Maybe think about the language you'll use to talk about your plan. None of those **inspirational** speeches that Yellows and Reds love. Keep to the facts, and be clear. Set reasonable goals. And be careful to avoid any dramatic body language.

Facts are the only things that matter

Details are essential to communicating with a Blue, and you must be exact. Mistakes or ignoring the details won't be welcome. Remember that it's not about whether the details are essential for a particular decision or not. A Blue decision-maker simply wants to know, and know exactly.

Conclusion: Prepare yourself well. When you think you're prepared and that you know all there is to know about an issue, go through it all one more time. Make sure you have answers to absolutely everything.

And accept that this person might want to have more information before moving on.

Only quality will do

Quality is what drives a Blue. Everything else comes second. He believes that things must always be done the correct way.

This, of course, takes a lot of time. But if you do it right from the beginning, you'll avoid having to redo it. This is actually a great way of saving time, although a Blue may not even consider this.

Conclusion: Be very careful in your work for a Blue. Don't **criticize** the Blue about how much time he spends on quality. Let the Blue understand that you're doing quality work and that you understand its value.

How to behave when you meet a Blue

A Blue has feelings like everyone else, and he values people. It just looks a little different. He may seem a little cold or not interested in other people. He's simply focused on the issue.

If we're trying to solve something, then this is a good approach. But every time other people, particularly Yellows or Greens, are involved, Blue behavior can be a problem. He simply doesn't realize that other people don't function in the same way. People want to feel like they can relate to this person.

Conclusion: Remind him that other people have feelings. Explain that he doesn't need to be critical all the time. Show him that people can be hurt when others criticize them. Being honest isn't an excuse for being unpleasant.

Rome wasn't built in a day!

We can tell Blues to hurry up, but they won't listen. Often Blues slow down even more when they're stressed. It's better to avoid having to fix things, which takes time. But sometimes things are urgent. You have to speed up in order to stay in the race. Blue is quite unmoved. He works at his own speed without worrying.

Conclusion: Calmly and carefully tell the Blue he'll need to work faster. Explain exactly why this is important. Point to the big picture.

"If it's in the book, it must be true."

Even Blues have feelings for what might be right, but they don't trust them because they can be wrong. For a Blue, the only thing that matters is the facts. And even the facts might not be enough—there may be more information out there that would change everything!

Conclusion: Tell your Blue friend that if he has to make a decision without all the facts, he can follow his feelings. Prove that sometimes it's better to do something rather than nothing, while waiting for more information. Point out that it can be logical to use feelings when you don't have all the facts. Explain that the results will still be good, and help him to calculate risk and to move on.

Decisions made here

Because the Blue experiences the decision itself as less important than the path to the decision, he can become inactive. You can help with this by leading him in the right direction or, in any case, in a direction.

Conclusion: Provide the Blue decision-maker with the information he needs. Push him to make a choice. Remind him about time and the effect of not making a decision. Explain that everything has been considered and all the risks have been removed.

In conclusion

Now you have some basic information about how to interact with the different colors. The first step is to try to understand others and then adapt to them. In this way, you gain their trust, and they're able to recognize themselves in you.

How difficult this is depends on what color you are, how well you know yourself, and how much you want to make progress with people in your everyday life.

CHAPTER EIGHT

How to deliver feedback

The challenges of speaking your mind

Who looks forward to bad news? No one. And yet, every now and then, we need to break bad news. Reds do this best; they'll just come out, say it, and then move on.

However, **feedback** is difficult to give and receive. When delivered badly, it will leave you feeling sick. The solution for many managers seems to be not to give any feedback. We don't know how to give either positive or negative feedback, so we ignore it.

There are many wrong ways to give positive or negative feedback. Negative feedback is usually the most difficult. If you can manage to deliver that, then you can probably manage the positive. The following advice works just as well for your private life as for your work life. The only thing you need to know is what color it's aimed at.

How to give feedback to a Red

Good news: you don't need any great skill to give negative feedback to a Red. The only thing you need is some personal protection because the temperature in the room will rise. If a Red doesn't respond to what you say, you should worry. Either he's ignoring you and what you're saying, or he's seriously ill.

When you're criticizing a Red, don't gift wrap it. It's enough of a challenge to get through to him because he always believes that he's right and you're wrong. Give real examples. Although Reds are efficient at getting things done, they can also be quick to blame others. Break things into tiny pieces and give examples.

Keep to the facts. A Red is not interested in people's feelings. As he prefers facts and sees himself as an excellent problem solver, make him the key to solving the problem.

By refusing to accept a Red's bad behavior, you can manage his anger and deliver your feedback. Gradually, he'll learn that he has to control himself.

Giving feedback to a Red looks like a violent argument, so it's important to pause if you're going to make progress. Do this by asking the Red to repeat what you've both agreed on.

Conclusion: Try not to give negative feedback to a Red if you're not feeling strong that day. Prepare yourself extremely well. You need to be full of self-confidence, so choose your time carefully. A Red is always strong, always full of self-confidence, so for him it doesn't matter. Be careful, as he might start accusing you of different things that make him feel like he's won the argument.

How to give feedback to a Yellow

Yellows would change things all the time if they could. So you would think that accepting feedback can be a way to start improving things. But this isn't how it works with Yellows. They're only in favor of change if it's their idea. Criticism from the outside isn't always well received. In giving negative feedback to a Yellow, you need to make a plan and follow it. Then give very real examples of behavior.

It's important to get him to recognize and accept the message.

If you don't recognize a problem, you don't need to solve it. However, be aware that he might not really be listening.

Criticizing a Yellow is difficult because he takes things personally and defends himself strongly. He thinks you've suddenly become enemies. So you have to explain that you don't dislike him—only his behavior. Ask the Yellow to repeat what you've agreed, and follow up as soon as you can. You might have to follow up several times to make sure he has really made a change.

Conclusion: Despite their flexibility and creativity, Yellows are actually the most difficult to change. They don't listen and only make changes that they themselves have thought of.

Their short memories also apply to bad feelings. Although they feel awful when criticized, they soon forget. They simply ignore everything that is difficult or unpleasant. So if you can just accept the complaining and the upset, you can continue toward your goal. By patiently never giving up, you'll eventually succeed.

How to give feedback to a Green

Criticizing a Green can be cruel. They'll feel bad and will simply shut down. In general, they'll think less of themselves and can be more **self-critical**.

There's a difference between being self-critical and changing, and self-critical and doing nothing about it. Many Greens go through life wishing that things were different. But they rarely do anything about it, and they continue to be unhappy. Sometimes it's a way to get some attention, to gain some power.

There are Greens who control everything and everyone in their families by simply refusing to do anything. Experts call this being passive-aggressive.

If you need to give feedback to a Green, here are some methods that might work.

Give real examples and use a gentle approach. The difference between Greens and both previous colors is that a Green actually listens. He hears what you're saying and dislikes it. Relationships are important to a Green, and he doesn't like to offend. You can explain how a certain type of behavior makes you sad, angry, or just generally upset. A Green person will understand, if you're honest about it.

You'll see how a Green falls apart, the more you give him negative criticism, but it's important not to say things like, "Maybe it's not that bad." Be clear, and go straight to the point. A hand on someone's shoulder can be enough to say, "We're still friends, but I have a problem when you do this or that."

A Green will accuse himself of being all kinds of stupid things when you tell him how you feel about his behavior. You might not be able to avoid him feeling upset and sorry. As with Yellows, dealing with a Green is like dealing with young children. The risk is that the negative feedback will damage your relationship with him. But you can solve this by quickly giving him good news and positive feedback. In this case, it's not enough just to say that you're only concerned about one issue. You need to show, not just say, that everything is going to be OK.

Greens don't always write down what you say to them, so it's a good idea to check with them to make sure you've both understood the conversation the same way.

We often think that others will behave the same way we would in any particular situation. Greens can be quite unclear when they speak to others, and often avoid talking about the real problem. They never go straight to the point themselves, so they imagine you haven't, either. Agree what the problem is and follow up. We're talking about changing something and creating a new way of behaving. And, as usual, Greens will try to solve the problem by doing . . . nothing. Make sure that doesn't happen!

Conclusion: You may feel guilty about giving negative feedback strongly to Greens. Make sure they don't use your guilt and uncertainty as an excuse not to change their behavior. You need to stand up and deliver the negative feedback—even to the friendly Greens in your life.

How to give feedback to a Blue

Before you try to give negative feedback to a Blue, make sure you know what you're talking about. A Blue knows exactly what he's done, and he has a much better eye for details than you do. So make sure you have your facts ready before the thought even enters your mind. The biggest task is finding out the details of what happened before you give any feedback.

It may be a good idea to check things with other people. The Blue will always have proof that what he did was correct—after all, that's why he did it. If it had been wrong, he wouldn't have done it.

It's not good enough to say things like, "I think you're working too slowly; can you please hurry up?" That's too general for a Blue. The words "working too slowly" don't really mean anything. What you need to do is point to accurate examples with details. Say things like, "The latest project took sixteen and a half hours too long." Then add up the effects this has had. "We can't charge the customer for those sixteen and a half hours, which means that the profit has now fallen by . . ."

This is a message that a Blue might consider because it uses details. However, it would be risky to present it in a conversation. You need to have everything written down. Blues don't really trust people who talk too much. The written word immediately becomes more true in their eyes.

So write down what you want to say, but check everything. And why not actually ask someone else to check the numbers before booking your meeting with the Blue?

A Yellow and a Green boss could easily put a hand on a Blue's shoulder when planning to give some tough negative feedback. This is the worst way to **approach** a Blue. He'll lose trust and won't listen the way you want him to. You should think about how a Red would do things. He would get straight to the point.

If you want to communicate with a Blue, you need to keep to the facts. Each time you start feeling guilty about saying negative things and start saying positive things, you'll confuse him. Remember that he's not there to be your friend, he's there to do a job.

It's reasonable to give him the chance to ask some questions about what you've said. You might not be able to answer all his questions, so you must simply decide how deep you want to go.

Ask the Blue to repeat what you've said, and follow up soon after. He needs to agree that he has seen and heard the same things you have. It's very likely that he'll be able to repeat everything precisely, but it's just as likely that he hasn't properly understood the message if you were unclear at all.

He understands that he should repeat what he knows you want to hear him say. But this isn't the same thing as him believing your negative feedback was important.

Conclusion: It's difficult to criticize a perfectionist. He already knows the best method, and he won't change his opinion. So it's all about doing your homework very well.

Remember that, although it may be difficult to get a Blue to respond to feedback, he has no problem criticizing others. He sees all the mistakes everyone else makes and he'll likely point out your mistakes when you least expect it. Not because he's being unpleasant, but just because you've made some.

CHAPTER NINE

Good color combinations & written communication

Groups of different colors

To work best, a group should have all colors in it. The Yellow has a new idea, the Red makes the decision, the Green does all the work, and the Blue evaluates and makes sure that the results are excellent. But often we find Yellows in positions better suited to Reds. Or, in the worst cases, they've been able to talk their way into a job that actually requires Blue behavior. Different people are inspired by different things, and that can cause them to move away from their core behavior.

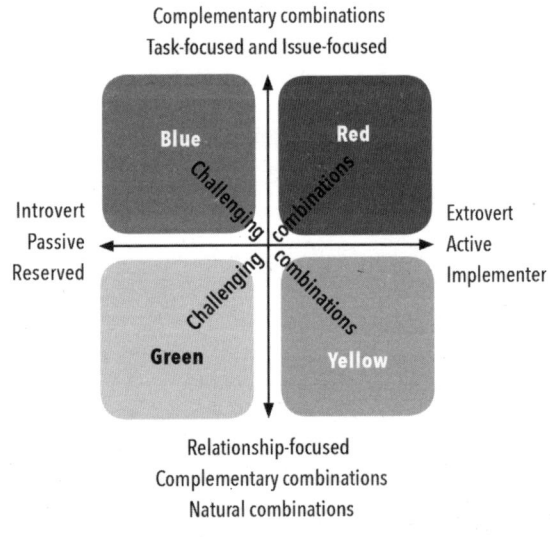

Group color combinations

So how do you put your team together? Look at the figure opposite. As you can see, different colors work differently together. If no one in the group has any knowledge of their behavior pattern, some colors will naturally work well together. For example, it's generally easier for two people to work together if they've the same **sense** of time, and work at a similar speed.

Natural combinations

If we look at the figure, we can see that Blue and Green could be a suitable combination, without much of an effort from either of them. They would certainly recognize each other's ability to breathe calmly and to think twice before doing something. Since both are introverts, each of them feels safe with the other. It's the same kind of energy. They don't stress but go into things deeply. They may find it difficult to make decisions, but the decisions that they do make will probably be well thought out.

Similarly, Red and Yellow work smoothly together, since they both want to act quickly and move forward. Here we also have the same kind of energy, only a different type. Both are powerful and confident, and because both are **verbal**, they find the right words. Certainly, they'll have a different focus in the conversation, but the conversation will still move. Both set high goals and think quickly. A team of Yellows and Reds will move fast, and while they're both clear about what they want, they'll inspire those around them to achieve great things. A Red can perceive a Yellow as being too talkative, but since neither of them is a great listener, they'll both just ignore the other when it suits them.

Complementary combinations

It also works to make pairs based on each color's focus. Both Blues and Reds are task-focused. Reds are certainly more interested in the result than in the process itself, and Blues are more concerned with the process and can ignore the result—but they're at least speaking the same language. Both do the work without chatting. They would **complement** each other in a good way.

Similarly, there's some logic in placing a Green with a Yellow. The speed at which they work will be different, but both believe that people are important. While one likes to relax, the other likes having fun. They'll easily find a similar focus. The Green will allow the Yellow to take as much space as he wants. One talks; the other listens. In addition, Greens are good at calming Yellows, who sometimes have a hard time focusing. Of course, there's a risk that they'll fail to spend enough time on the work itself, but they'll have a good time. As both can find it difficult to say no, it might also be a good idea to avoid trusting them with too much money.

Real problems

It would be quite a challenge to put a Red and a Green together. If the task depends on **cooperation**, then issues will quickly come out. In the beginning, the Green is very passive, particularly when compared to the Red, who gets going even before he's heard the instructions.

The Red will be very critical when the Green complains about the amount of work. At the same time, the Green thinks that the Red is aggressive and never listens. However, it may work out. A Green is prepared to **cooperate**; that's his strength. So there can be a certain logic in setting a Red with a Green. A Red likes giving orders, and a Green is usually OK with receiving them.

According to William Moulton Marston's theories, published in his 1928 work *Emotions of Normal People* (see Chapter 11), the greatest challenge of all is to ask a Yellow and a Blue to work together. If neither of them knows how their personalities work, there will be conflict from the start. The Yellow starts the task without any idea what to do or how to do it. He doesn't read any instructions, and he doesn't listen long enough to find out what the task is actually about. He'll talk about what an exciting project they've been given. Meanwhile, the Blue starts reading and researching all the material available. He doesn't say a word but just sits there and thinks.

The Yellow will consider him boring. The Blue will be disturbed by the Yellow's nonstop chat. He'll slowly begin to get annoyed. He believes that the Yellow just talks and doesn't deserve his attention. And when the Yellow finally realizes that he hasn't won the Blue over to his side, he'll talk even more. Finally, in the worst case, they'll sit in their own corners, both mad for different reasons. The only solution is for them to learn about themselves.

Go Green!

It's not easy to read and understand everyone. If a person only has one color, then it will be obvious what you should do. A person who is only Red or only Yellow is hard to miss. But even the true Greens or Blues are quite easy to identify if you know what to look for.

Only about 5 per cent of the population has just one color in their behavior. Around 80 per cent have two, and the rest have three. No one has four, not with the tool that I use.

It's also quite easy to recognize people who have two colors. Two-color combinations are normally: Blue/Red, Red/Yellow, Yellow/Green, or Green/Blue. It does happen, of course, that opposite qualities can be found in the same person. There are lots of Yellow/Blue people. There's nothing wrong with that; it's just less common. But what's really unusual is Red/Green combinations.

If someone is very difficult to read, it may be because he has three colors. Then the situation will determine his behavior. If you really can't analyze the person you meet, just listen. Simply act Green if you're unsure. People sometimes say they can't understand a person because he doesn't do anything. But even a person who is very passive shows some kind of behavior. A person who doesn't do much—that's Blue behavior.

Written communication

Many things are revealed in the way we write. Different colors write in different ways; some take the time to say what they want, while others keep it short. If you read through a longer piece of writing, such as a report or a letter, you'll have lots of information.

If the only thing you have is an email, then look at it closely. Is it full of facts? Is it personal? Is it short, or does it seem to have been written quickly and without much thought? All of these little details are important signs that you can use.

From: 57ristian.jonsson@teamcommunication.com
To: Cina.cinasson@coco.net
Subject: Meeting

Meeting tomorrow morning at 11. BE ON TIME!
- K

What do you think? Is K screaming because he used capital letters? It's not clear. It could be that he just wanted to say that the time for the meeting is important. It doesn't matter to him that the person receiving the email might not like the shortness and the capitals. As always, a Red can live with that. He just wanted to be clear.

Your action: Reply immediately! Be short and direct. Simply reply, "OK."

Even in writing, a Yellow is very immediate and relaxed. He likes to share stories and keep things personal. There's a lot of chat and a good laugh to attract your attention.

From: 57ristian.jonsson@teamcommunication.com
To: Cina.cinasson@coco.net
Subject: Meeting

Hello, Cina! What's up? Were you at the game last night? I saw Lasse was there. He poured his drink all over himself, and I thought that I would never stop laughing! Look at the picture I put on Facebook. By the way, I thought that we could sit down and chat about that customer tomorrow morning before lunch if it works for you. Is eleven o'clock OK?
Ciao! Krille

From: 57ristian.jonsson@teamcommunication.com
To: Cina.cinasson@coco.net
Subject: Meeting

Oh, I forgot to attach the photo. Here it is.
Krille

Your reply? There isn't any need to rush, but do respond or he'll worry. Be friendly as well. Don't forget to thank him for the picture and mention that you laughed at his story.

A softer, more personal Green email. Kristian checked this email, to make sure there was nothing challenging in it. Reminding people about meetings that were booked a long time previously can be perceived as slightly rude by some people, so here he wants to be sure that nothing can be misunderstood.

From: 57ristian.jonsson@teamcommunication.com
To: Cina.cinasson@coco.net
Subject: Meeting

I just wanted to remind you about the meeting tomorrow at eleven. Hope it still works for you. I'm going to bring in some homemade cake to have with our coffee. Have a good one!
With kind regards, Kristian

And how do you respond to this friendly email? Be personal and pleasant in return. Say thank you, maybe also for the cake.

From: 57ristian.jonsson@teamcommunication.com
To: Cina.cinasson@coco.net
Subject: Meeting

Good morning, Christina.

Ahead of tomorrow's meeting with our client, I would appreciate it if you could become familiar with the necessary information.

I've attached three documents.

Greetings,

Kristian Jonsson

The original invitation to the meeting was sent out a long time ago, but an alarm was probably set on his computer to send out an email to remind people about the meeting a day before. The email contains facts and nothing personal. There's a little note reminding you that it's best to be well prepared.

What's the best way to answer this Blue email? Say that you've received it with the files. Say that you'll ask if you have any questions after reading through the information. And know that you should read the whole thing carefully.

CHAPTER TEN
Anger and stress

What makes us mad?

Anger is a good way to judge a person's color. What upsets one person may not upset someone else. By observing how someone reacts when things do not go the right way, you get important clues.

"I'm surrounded by idiots!"

It doesn't take much for a Red to get angry. Remember that, of all the colors, they're the ones most often surrounded by idiots, so there are many reasons to be annoyed.

A Red's strength is that when they explode, they lose all the anger they've been feeling. It's quick and doesn't last long. He says what he wants to say, and then he moves on. Sure, he can leave many confused people around him, but that's their problem. Then something upsetting happens again, and he just explodes. And again. And again.

Many perceive a Red's moods as totally unpredictable. He can explode at any time. But if you know the Red, you probably also know what makes him angry.

However, it's important to know that a Red doesn't consider himself an angry person. He's just told someone what he thinks, or shouted at him. It's just a way of communicating. But to a Green, it might seem that a Red is angry even when he's just sharing his opinion. It's common that many people simply back away, to avoid the Red's anger. By showing their anger, Reds miss out on a lot of feedback.

"I'm very upset! Do you even hear what I'm saying?"

Even the cheerful Yellow gets angry, although they're generally sunny and optimistic. Like Reds, they're active, **perceptive** people. This means that they've a lot to react to. And if you're quick-thinking, and you sometimes get excited, things can happen. You'll know they're getting angry, but it happens gradually. A Yellow will feel guilty if he gets angry with someone close to him: colleague, family member, or neighbor. So he'll make an extra effort to be kind the next time they meet. He'll feel bad, unlike a Red.

If a person is a combination of Red and Yellow, things can get tough, depending on the reason the person is angry. True Yellows can let their own importance get in the way most of the time. However, they've such bad memories that they forget about it quickly.

Be careful of the anger of a patient man

You may never have seen a Green get angry, but that doesn't mean it won't happen. It just means that instead of their anger turning out, it turns in.

Many Greens receive and accept without complaining because they want to avoid conflict, but also because they can't say no. Agreeing is easier. This doesn't mean that Greens don't have their own opinions. They just don't talk about them. A Green accepts one perceived wrong after the other.

Greens don't let out anger but control their emotions so as not to create trouble or bring attention to themselves. But they feel and experience as much as everyone else. They just can't let it out. But we can help them. We can ask questions, invite them in, and look at their body language for signs. Create a healthy environment around a Green for him to be comfortable enough to say what he thinks so that he doesn't have to agree all the time. Or he'll turn all his anger in, and we know what this kind of stress can do to a person.

Complain about something every day

Blues have less need to communicate than Greens. So they don't do it. Even Blues can focus too much on themselves, but they've a system to keep stress under control.

A Blue's anger comes out in small complaints. His anger is real, but he'll argue about things rather than doing something about them. He complains that others should see what he sees, he doesn't have any power to act, or he's simply in a bad mood. But for him, this is a great way of keeping the stress under control.

The way to deal with this is to ask for examples and suggestions for improvement. Maybe the Blue has solved the problem that is worrying him, but he needs a straight question for him to step forward and suggest a solution.

What can you do about the fact that people get angry differently?

With these simple **observations** in mind, you can quickly form an idea of what type of person you're dealing with. Watch how he reacts under stress. But remember these suggestions only apply to single colors. The more important a particular thing is for a person, the stronger his reaction will be.

Stress factors and energy thieves

Anger is one thing. Stress is another. Sometimes one leads to the other, but not always. Some people become angry because of stress; others become stressed because of anger. When we speak about stress, we often mean the feeling of having too much to do and too little time to do it. However, the stress that makes us truly suffer is often due to other things. If you expect a lot from yourself, you can become stressed, even if you have enough time.

You may find it difficult to sleep or may feel pain in your body. This feeling of stress comes when we experience greater demands and expectations than we can cope with.

Different people react differently to stress

Different people can experience the same event in different ways, and a person can experience similar events differently at different times. The things you have been through in the past and how you're feeling right now all affect how you act and react.

If you're not tired and feel well, a tough week at work can be seen as a positive challenge. But if you're tired and feeling down, you may experience the same week as something horrible.

How does your color affect your stress? It says nothing about how much stress you can bear. But it can say something about what stresses you, and how you'll react to stress. Once you've understood what the most important stress factors in your life are, you'll be better able to avoid them when possible.

If you're a manager responsible for a number of people and you know their behavior types, you can avoid the worst stress and the worst problems, which is good for the group's work.

Don't take everything you read in the rest of this chapter too seriously!

Stress factors for Reds

If you would like to stress out a Red, you can try one of the following:

- Don't involve him in any decision-making
- Don't achieve any results
- Remove any kind of challenge
- Waste time and **resources** and work as inefficiently as possible
- Make sure that everything becomes a routine
- Make a lot of stupid mistakes
- Give him no control over others
- Tell him often to cool down or to lower his voice.

What does a Red do when he gets stressed?

He blames everyone else. As a Red is often surrounded by idiots, it's easy for him to find people to blame.

Reds are always more demanding than other colors. They expect a lot from themselves, and they expect a lot from you. When under stress, they're very demanding and driven—much more than usual.

The Red will shut out his colleagues. He becomes closed, focuses on the task at hand, and works even harder. Remember that his anger is quick, so be careful what you do in his presence.

Can I help Reds manage their stress?

If you have the power to give a direct order, ask him to control himself. It actually works. Another way to make it easier for Reds in stressful situations is to send them home and tell them to do some physical exercise—anything to burn some of that energy. Send them to a place where they can run in some kind of competition, spending their energy on winning. When they come back, most of their aggression will have disappeared.

Stress factors for Yellows

If you would like to get a Yellow to feel stress, try one of the following:
- Pretend you can't see him
- Don't believe what he says
- Make work as **routine** as possible
- Keep him away from the rest of the group
- Make clear that he mustn't joke at work
- Push him to think carefully before doing things—twice
- Argue about silly little things
- Give him negative feedback in public.

What does a Yellow do when he gets stressed?

Be prepared for the fact that he'll draw attention to himself even more than usual—he'll talk too much and force himself into the center of everything.

He also risks becoming excessively and unrealistically optimistic. You've never experienced a real challenge until you've tried to cope with a stressed Yellow. He'll develop plans that are so wild that not even he can believe them.

Can I help Yellows manage their stress?

Let a Yellow organize a party. He needs to meet people in social situations. He can fall very far if he remains under stress for too long. When things are at their worst, suggest doing something fun and make sure he enjoys himself for a while!

Stress factors for Greens

If you, for any reason, would like to get a Green to feel stress, I suggest the following:
- Take every safe thing away from him
- Leave lots of open ends
- Be with him all the time
- Make fast and unexpected changes
- Ask him, "Would you please do the whole thing again?"
- Tell him, "Look here! We can't agree on absolutely everything."
- Bring attention to him.

What does a Green do when he gets stressed?

He becomes very reserved and almost cold. His body language becomes stiff and closed. If you're responsible for his stress, he won't want to be near you. Some Greens become cold and distant even toward people they care very much about.

They also become very uncertain. Stress makes Greens afraid of making mistakes. If a child gets sick at home, a Green becomes passive and just looks on because he's afraid of doing the wrong thing. He'll also blame himself for the situation and may become completely closed.

At work, it may be slightly different. Many Greens can become very stubborn, refusing to change anything. Even when they see that a particular method isn't working well, they can refuse to act.

Can I help Greens manage their stress?

Allow them to do nothing. Give them free time for things like gardening, sleep, or other relaxation. Maybe something like sending them to see a movie—not with a large group of people, but possibly on their own—or giving them a good book that takes two days to read.

They don't really want to do anything. Let them do nothing until the stress disappears. Then they'll be back to normal.

Stress factors for Blues

If you want to get a Blue to feel stress, just upset his calculations.

- Tell him, "You don't know what you're talking about."
- Get the management team to make a sudden decision
- Tell him, "This could be risky or uncertain, but we're going to do it anyway."
- Surprise him with something like, "Your wife's parents are coming over unexpectedly! Fantastic!"

- Say, "Whoops! What happened here?"
- Tell him, "Forget about the rules. Let's invent!"
- Remind him, "We simply need to take bigger risks."
- Surround him with very emotional people.

What does a Blue do when he gets stressed?

He becomes extremely pessimistic. It gets even worse than usual. Suddenly, everything becomes black, and he becomes very low. He often doesn't want to do anything, and nothing is of interest any more.

He also gets impossibly precise. When they feel stress, many people move faster. Not a Blue. He puts on the brakes. Now isn't the time for making any mistakes. Those around him can expect a lot of criticism. He'll suddenly point out every little mistake he observes. He might also become a terrible know-it-all.

Can I help Blues manage their stress?

Blues must be given time and space to think. They want to analyze the situation and understand the connections, and they need to be given time to do that. If you give them space, they'll come back—eventually. But if they feel too stressed, you may need to offer them more active help.

Conclusion: What can we learn from studying different people under stress?

A Red becomes even tougher and more aggressive, a Yellow becomes down and wilder, a Green becomes more passive and uncertain than usual, and a Blue can become completely closed and precise.

The most important thing is to avoid stressing people unnecessarily. Of course, you knew that already, but it can be helpful to understand what actually causes stress for each type. To push a Red is not as stressful as pushing a Green or a Blue. In fact, you have to push a Red, or he would just get bored.

The situation, your behavior type, the time of day, the level of work, the group, the weather—lots of things cause stress in our lives. But if you give your attention to all these things, the situation will work out perfectly.

CHAPTER ELEVEN
History

What's behind this book?

There has always been a need to put people in groups. When the Stone Age finished and we became more thoughtful, we discovered that all over the world people were different.

But how different are people really? And how have those differences been described? Here are some examples.

The Greeks

Hippocrates, who lived four centuries before Christ, is considered the father of medicine. Unlike many other doctors of that time, he believed that disease came from nature and not from the gods. Hippocrates believed that there are four types of person: choleric, sanguine, phlegmatic, and melancholic.

A choleric person sometimes frightens those around him with his powerful ways. "Choleric" can be translated as "hot-blooded."

A sanguine person is controlled by the blood, by the heart. Creative and happy, he spreads positive energy around him. He's optimistic and cheerful.

A phlegmatic person is inactive and slow in movement.

Finally, a melancholic person is sad and dark.

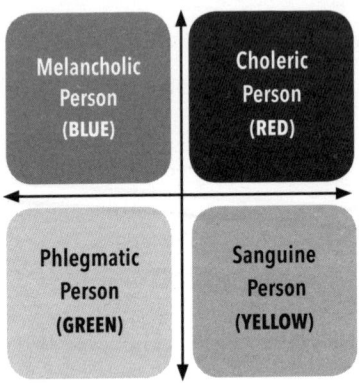

Hippocrates's types

The Aztecs

The Aztecs were a people who lived in Central Mexico from the fourteenth century to the sixteenth century. They're known for their advanced society and buildings.

When they tried to divide people into different groups, they used something they knew well—the four **elements**: fire, air, earth, and water. To this day, the four elements are used to describe different conditions of mind. Nobody really knows if the Aztecs were the first to think of this idea, but we do know that they used it.

Fire people were fiery and ready to explode. They were soldiers who fought to get their own way, and leaders.

Air people were different. They were also strong but a lot more relaxed. They entered like an amazing wind, kicking up a little dirt in the process.

Earth people worked for the village, for the whole group. They were stable and brought safety. They were there to create things, to build for the future.

Aztecs had respect for water, as it can destroy everything in its path but you can also bottle it—if you know how to. Quiet and safe, water people observed everything.

These are similar to Hippocrates's theories, but with different names.

The Aztec elements

William Moulton Marston

In 1928, William Moulton Marston published his work *Emotions of Normal People*, in which he studied the differences in the behavior of healthy people. This provided the **inspiration** for what became known as DISC, which this book is based on. A few years after discovering Marston's work (in the 1950s), Walter Clarke developed DISC using Marston's observations.

As you've seen, DISC is a tool used to put the different types of human behavior in groups. A lot of work has been done since

Marston's days, and, over the years, many other people have been involved in improving DISC.

Marston found a way to show how people were different. He noted particular differences between personalities. Nowadays, we use the following:

- Dominance produces activity in an unfriendly environment.
- Inspiration produces activity in a favorable environment.
- Stability produces passivity in a favorable environment.
- **Compliance** produces passivity in an unfriendly environment.

The four letters D, I, S, and C (Dominance, Inspiration, Stability, and Compliance) form DISC, which is used throughout the world.

The dominance characteristic in any person tells you how he approaches problems and deals with challenges.

Inspiration applies to a person who will always be able to convince others. You could say that dominance is about acting, and inspiration is about interacting.

Stability is measured by how open a person is to change. A strong need for stability means a person doesn't want change, while someone who enjoys change will have a lower need for stability. This leads, of course, to a number of different behaviors—like wanting to go back to the "good old days" for example.

Finally, compliant ability shows how ready someone is to follow rules. Of course, this also produces certain characteristics that are linked. Here we find those who can't accept that things go wrong.

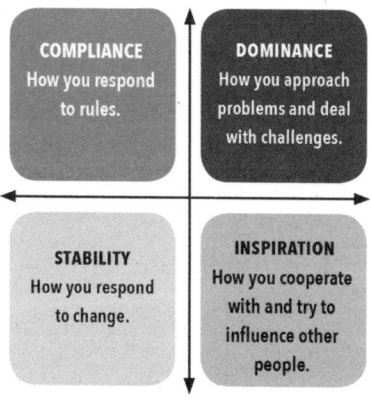

The DISC tool

You've probably noticed that for all these systems, these behavior characteristics are all linked to a color. The colors aren't essential; they're only a way to make sense of and learn about the system more easily.

Marston finished researching this topic in the 1930s. Many others have used his research and developed a tool that has been used by nearly 50 million people in the past thirty-five years.

But it's always helpful to remember that though in theory there's no difference between ideas and practice, in the real world there's a big difference. Not least, that most people are a combination of two colors.

A final example from everyday life

A few years ago, I did an experiment with a group of managers. They were professional and clever, and all of them had successful careers.

I divided the managers into behavior color groups: Red, Yellow, Green, and Blue. They had to solve a problem that was connected to their work and required cooperation. They were given an hour to complete it. I explained the challenge and all the groups enthusiastically got to work.

After they had been working for a while, I went around and checked what was going on in the various teams.

In the Red Group, the noise level was high. Three people were standing and loudly explaining why they were right. Two of them were in the middle of an argument, while the final person had decided to work alone. Completely ignoring the shouting, he was writing something really fast. When I asked if everything was OK, they stopped and looked at me in surprise.

"Great!" one guy said without smiling. "We're almost done here."

I left them and continued on to the Yellow Group, which was also working energetically. The discussions were lively, with everyone trying to convince the others of their own position.

While the Reds were angry with one another, there was nothing but smiles here. Three of the Yellows were trying to use the whiteboard, and another told me an amusing story that had nothing to do with the task. The fifth manager in the Yellow Group was drawing on a piece of paper and sending emails on his phone.

Next, I visited the Green Group. Inside the room, it was calm. Their voices were quiet, and they were all listening rather than speaking. The main goal was stability and safety. Five of the managers were sitting quietly, listening to one of their colleagues telling a sad story about a dog.

The last manager had written some suggestions about how they could solve the task I'd given them, but every suggestion ended with a question mark. She needed more help, and it looked like she would have to ask for it.

In the last room, the Blue Group was incredibly quiet. A lot of thought was happening, but there was no real communication. A woman was reading silently through the task with her lips moving. I asked if they needed help to get started and got a few uncertain nods in reply. They soon began a very thorough discussion. It was obvious that they were on the right track, but in incredible detail.

I remember taking a look at the clock. Half the time I had given them was over, but they hadn't really produced anything. They were more interested in doing things correctly than in getting things done. I left them and went back to the large hall. Before the whole time was up, the Red Group arrived, looking pleased with themselves. They were happy to be the first back. They'd clearly won the test.

I had to go and get all the other groups. The Yellow Group was the slowest. Two of them were talking on their phones, and another manager needed some coffee and cake before returning.

When all the groups were back, I let them present their work.

The Red Group presented like winners. They'd turned the task into a race. They were ready in thirty minutes, even though they had an hour. The rest of the time they'd spent phoning their colleagues, checking what they were doing with their time. It was a good presentation, well-organized, and well thought out. But about thirty seconds into the report, it was clear that the Red Group had solved a completely different problem than the one I'd given them.

When I asked if they had actually read the instructions, they all began arguing. One of the men stated confidently that they'd adapted the task to **reality**. He expected us to applaud them. When it didn't happen, they returned to their seats. A second after sitting down, the woman in the group began playing with her phone. A message had to be sent immediately.

After that, it was the Yellow Group: three women and two men. All of them smiled and stood at the front. Who should begin? After a short argument, a woman came to the front and presented the exciting discussions they'd had for the past hour.

She spoke for a while about the whole thing being an inspirational exercise; she described how she was going to use what they'd learned when she returned to her work. Her presentation was fun, and everyone laughed. I was also amused by the woman's story, but its only purpose was to hide the fact that the group hadn't solved the task. However, the Yellow

Group was applauded, mostly because people enjoyed their presentation.

Now it was time for the Green Group. It took a while to get everyone up on stage. The Yellow Group had argued about who was going first, but in the Green Group at least half of their six people looked ill. This was one of the larger groups, but they were all nervous.

After a moment, one of the men began to speak. He faced the whiteboard most of the time. He talked softly, turning toward the members of his team for support and most of the message was lost.

The Green Group hadn't solved the task, even though they had made more progress than the Yellow Group. I asked if everyone in the group agreed with the presentation. He said that he thought that most of them agreed with most of it. I asked the group, and they all nodded, but at least four of them looked unhappy and had their arms crossed tightly, which seemed to say the opposite.

Finally, the Blue Group came up in line and stood in alphabetical order, as they had agreed. Arne went through the instructions, saying that there were several points that had made the task challenging. Among other things, he said the language was not always clear and there were mistakes on the first page.

Then it was Berit's turn to go through the basic ideas of their work, after being interrupted twice by Arne, who believed that a few details needed explaining. When Kjell took over, they still weren't even close to providing a solution to the problem. Stefan didn't make anything clearer. When Yolanda finally said they needed more time to really finish the task, everybody in the hall started talking.

The Red Group quickly called the Blue Group complete idiots, the Yellow Group felt it was the most boring thing they'd ever experienced, and the Green Group just suffered silently.

Conclusions

The purpose of the whole exercise was to show that no group should only have the same personality type. The best way to put a group of people together is by mixing different types of people. This is the only way to achieve good cooperation. However, most of the organizations I have worked with fail on this when they hire people. Managers bring in new people who are like themselves because they understand each other.

This book has been about explaining exactly why the groups in this example worked the way they did and giving you the tools to avoid similar problems in your own life. We're all different. If you keep your eyes open, you'll find out exactly how different. The rest is up to you.

During-reading questions

CHAPTER SIX

1 How does a Red typically walk?
2 What do some Yellows do, which some colors don't like?
3 What kind of voices do Greens often have?
4 What is the easiest way to describe a Blue's body language?

CHAPTER SEVEN

1 What do Reds find boring, and what effect can this have on their work?
2 What do Yellows deal badly with, and what should you do about this?
3 Why are most people unable to deal with change?
4 What does the writer mean when he says that "a Blue isn't interested in your personal tastes"?

CHAPTER EIGHT

1 List the main problems in giving negative feedback to each color.

CHAPTER NINE

1 Why might a Blue and a Green work well together?
2 Why might a Red and a Yellow work well together?
3 Which color combination is the greatest challenge of all? Why, and what will be the consequence?

CHAPTER TEN

1 What makes a Red stressed if removed, and what should you encourage him to do to relieve stress?

2 What makes a Yellow stressed if they are not allowed to do it, and what should you let him do to relieve stress?

3 What makes a Green stressed if you do it all the time, and what should you allow him to do to relieve stress?

4 What can you say to a Blue to make him stressed, and what must he be given to relieve stress?

CHAPTER ELEVEN

1 Which four types of person did Hippocrates believe that there were?

2 Which four elements did the Aztecs divide people into?

CONCLUSION

1 In the writer's experiment with a group of managers, which colors performed best and worst in your opinion?

After-reading questions

1 Which color will always prefer to be the leader of a project?

2 Which person would enjoy giving a speech the most?

3 Which person would know exactly where he saved that email from his boss?

4 Which person will remember personal criticism the longest?

5 Which combination of colors would make the best team?

6 Which color is most common in your social circle?

Exercises

1 **Write the correct words in your notebook.**

> slow   involve   connection   organize   alone
> calm   direct   control   future   past
> conflict   present   quick   caution
> change   routine

COMPLIANT (Blue)	**DOMINANT** (Red)
• _Slow_ reaction	• .... reaction
• Most effort to	• Most effort to ....
• Least interest in relationships	• Least interest for caution in relationships
• Focus on the	• Focus on the ....
• Acts with	• .... action
• Tries to avoid involvement	• Tries to avoid involvement
STABLE (Green)	**INSPIRING** (Yellow)
• .... reaction	• Very quick reaction
• Most effort for	• Most effort to ....
• Least interest in	• Least interest in ....
• Focus on the present	• Focus on the ....
• Acts to support other people	• Takes action quickly
• Tries to reject	• Tries to avoid being ....

2 **Who says or thinks this? Write R (Red), Y (Yellow), G (Green), or B (Blue) in your notebook.**

1 "Can I win something? In that case, I'm in." ....R....

2 "Excuse me, but that's not quite accurate."

3 "I know exactly what you mean."

4 "I know lots of people. All of them, in fact."

5 "If the path is different to the map, there's something wrong with the path."

6 "'Quick' is the same as 'good'."

7 "That sounds fun! Let me do it!"

8 "We don't want any unpleasant surprises."

CHAPTER FIVE

3 **Write the correct word in your notebook.**

1 So who decides what kind of **behave / _behavior_** is right and wrong?

2 Remember that **communicate / communication** usually depends on the listener.

3 Blues' **critic / critical** thinking can turn to not trusting and questioning those around them.

4 Reds are **perceived / perception** as tough, impatient, aggressive, and controlling.

5 They're unable to change, which others perceive as being afraid, **stubborn / stubbornness** , and cold.

6 The result? Even more **passive / passivity**.

4 Match the verbs and the nouns together. Then write sentences in your notebook.

Example: *1—f*

1	hearing	**a**	a movie
2	looking at	**b**	a presentation
3	watching	**c**	a talk
4	taking part	**d**	in a discussion
5	giving	**e**	pictures
6	doing	**f**	words

5 Are these sentences *true* or *false*? Write the correct answers in your notebook.

1 When something amazing or pleasant happens, many people put their hands up to their faces. ...*false*....
When something awful or unpleasant happens, many people put their hands up to their faces.

2 If you have a natural, relaxed, but not too relaxed posture, people often think you're self-confident.

3 When we listen carefully, we can move our heads to one side.

4 Anyone who presses too hard in a handshake is probably submissive but doesn't really want to be.

5 Holding your hands together in front of you often means power and a feeling of safety.

6 The personal area, when two people who know each other are communicating, is generally a few inches.

6 **Choose the correct words to replace the underlined words. Write them in your notebook.**

take your side	give up	throw you out
point out	keep up	take on

1 The second part deals with how you get people to <u>agree with you</u>. ...*take your side*...

2 He might <u>make you leave</u> if he thinks you're just trying to win him over.

3 <u>Show</u> the risks involved in hurrying.

4 Explain that others can't <u>go at the same speed</u>.

5 Don't <u>stop</u>.

6 Prove things with facts, and demand that he checks before deciding to <u>start</u> a new project.

CHAPTER EIGHT

7 **Complete these conditional sentences in your notebook.**

1 If a Red ...*doesn't respond*... (**not respond**) to what you say, you should worry.

2 Yellows would change things all the time if they .... (**can**).

3 If you .... (**need**) to give feedback to a Green, here are some methods that might work.

4 If it .... (**be**) wrong, he wouldn't have done it.

5 If you .... (**want**) to communicate with a Blue, you need to keep to the facts.

6 It's just as likely that he hasn't properly understood the message if you .... (**be**) unclear at all.

8 **Write the color of the people who wrote these emails (1–4) in your notebook.**

1 Email sent by a ....*Blue*....

> **From**: kristian.jonsson@teamcommunication.com
> **To**: Cina.cinasson@coco.net
> **Subject**: Meeting at 11.am
> Good morning, Christina.
> Ahead of tomorrow's meeting with our client, I would appreciate it if you could become familiar with the necessary information.
> I've attached three documents.
> Greetings,
> Kristian Jonsson

2 Email sent by a ....

> **From**: kristian.jonsson@teamcommunication.com
> **To**: Cina.cinasson@coco.net
> **Subject**: Meeting
> I just wanted to remind you about the meeting tomorrow at eleven. Hope it still works for you. I'm going to bring in some homemade cake to have with our coffee. Have a good one!
> With kind regards, Kristian

3 Email sent by a ....

> **From**: kristian.jonsson@teamcommunication.com
> **To**: Cina.cinasson@coco.net
> **Subject**: Meeting
> Meeting tomorrow morning at 11. BE ON TIME!
> - K

4 Email sent by a ....

> **From**: kristian.jonsson@teamcommunication.com
> **To**: Cina.cinasson@coco.net
> **Subject**: Meeting
> Hello, Cina! What's up? Were you at the game last night? I saw Lasse was there. He poured his drink all over himself, and I thought that I would never stop laughing! Look at the picture I put on Facebook. By the way, I thought that we could sit down and chat about that customer tomorrow morning before lunch if it works for you. Is eleven o'clock OK?
> Ciao! Krille
>
> Oh, I forgot to attach the photo. Here it is.
> Krille

CHAPTER TEN

9 **Which word is closest in meaning? Write the word in your notebook.**

1 strength   approach / ***power*** / value
2 perceptive   creative / direct / intelligent
3 conflict   argument / comparison / difference
4 observation   decision / thought / present
5 control   cooperate / communicate / dominate

CHAPTER ELEVEN

10 **Put these words into groups in the correct order in your notebook.**

> choleric   stability   fire   dominance   earth
> air   inspiration   melancholic   sanguine
> phlegmatic   compliance   water

The color system in this book	The Greeks	The Aztecs	DISC
Red	*choleric*	....	....
Yellow	....	....	....
Green	....	....	....
Blue	....	....	....

11 **Match the color with what the groups did in the author's experiment in your notebook.**

Example: *Red—c*

Red   **a**   The presentation was fun, and everyone laughed, but its only purpose was to hide the fact that the group hadn't solved the task.

Yellow   **b**   They came up in line and stood in alphabetical order. They went through the instructions, saying that there were several points that had made the task challenging, but they still weren't even close to providing a solution to the problem.

Green   **c**   They presented like winners. It was a good presentation, well-organized, and well thought out. But about thirty seconds into the report, it was clear that they had solved a completely different problem.

Blue   **d**   This was one of the larger groups, but they were all nervous. They hadn't solved the task, even though they had made more progress than some other groups.

Project work

1 Consider a well-known person who is typical of a color.
   You can use a person mentioned in the book or choose your
   own example. You should:
   • analyze their behavior based on the characteristics of their
     color
   • decide if they are totally Red, Yellow, Blue, or Green
   • consider if they have behavior relating to another color, too.

2 Write an email to a work colleague giving negative feedback
   about their behavior (e.g. always being late, interrupting
   people at meetings, poor people skills, being badly prepared).
   In your email, make sure you:
   • speak to the person in a way that their color will understand
   • give the negative feedback in a way that will make them
     change their behavior forever
   • make sure that you can continue having a good relationship
     with that person.

3 Create a class survey to find out which color your classmates
   are. In your survey consider:
   • what motivates them
   • what they are not interested in
   • their body language
   • how they see themselves
   • what stresses them
   • how they deal with criticism
   • how they behave in group situations.

Essay questions

1 What do you think about the writer's decision to only use he, his, and him in this book? (500 words)

2 According to the author of this book, most people are Green or a combination of two colors, and nobody has the characteristics of more than three colors. Do you agree? (500 words)

3 How do you think understanding your own behavior and the behavior of others can help you get along better in your social life and work life? (500 words)

An answer key for all questions and exercises can be found at **www.penguinreaders.co.uk**

Glossary

adapt (v.);
adaptable (adj.);
adaptation (n.)
If you *adapt* to a new or different situation, you change your *behavior* so that you can deal with it in a successful way. An *adaptable* person is able to *adapt* easily. *Adaptation* is the noun of *adapt*.

aggressive (adj.);
aggressively (adv.);
aggression (n.)
An *aggressive* person or animal is determined to get what they want or show how they feel, and often does this in an angry, unpleasant, and sometimes violent way. *Aggressively* is the adverb of *aggressive*. *Aggression* is angry, unpleasant, and sometimes violent *behavior* toward someone or something.

analyze (v.)
If you *analyze* something, you study it in detail in order to understand more about it.

applaud (v.)
to clap your hands to show that you like or approve of someone or something, for example a speech, show, concert, etc.

approach (n. and v.)
An *approach* is a way of doing something. To *approach* a problem, situation, etc. is to start to deal with it.

approachable (adj.)
An *approachable* person is friendly and easy to talk to.

assess (v.);
assessment (n.)
If you *assess* something or someone, you think about them carefully and decide what *characteristics* they have or how good they are. *Assessment* is the noun of *assess*.

attitude (n.)
how you feel or think about someone or something, and how this makes you behave

behavior (n.)
the way that a person or thing does something. *Behavior* is the noun of *behave*.

body language (n.)
when you *communicate* what you are thinking or feeling by the way that you move your body, instead of talking

CEO (n.)
Chief Executive Officer: the person who has the most important job in a company.

characteristic (n.)
something that is special about a person, animal, or thing—like parts of their personality, appearance, etc.

colleague (n.)
a person who you work with

common (adj.);
uncommon (adj.)
Something that is *common* happens
often or is experienced by most people in a certain situation. If it is not
uncommon for a thing to happen, then
this thing happens quite often.

communicate (v.);
communication (n.);
communicator (n.)
If you *communicate*, you share
information with another person or
animal by speaking, writing, or using
body language. *Communication* is the
noun of *communicate*. A person who
is a good *communicator* is very good at
communicating.

complement (v.);
complementary (adj.)
If two people or things *complement*
each other, or if they are *complementary*,
they are different but more useful or
attractive together.

complex (adj.)
A *complex* thing has a lot of different
parts and is difficult to understand.

compliance (n.)
compliant (adj.)
If you are *compliant*, you obey rules
or do what someone tells you to do.
This is *compliance*.

conflict (n.)
when people argue because they
don't agree or want different things

convince (v.)
to make someone believe that
something is true or that you are
right about something

cooperation (n.);
cooperate (v.)
If people *cooperate*, they work together
in order to achieve something.
Cooperation is the noun of *cooperate*.

core (adj.)
basic or most important

creative (adj.);
creativity (n.)
A *creative* person has lots of new ideas
and is good at producing things from
them. *Creativity* is the ability to think
of new ideas and produce new things.

critical thinking (n.)
when you *analyze* information in a
logical way in order to decide what
you think is true or correct

criticize (v.);
criticism (n.)
You *criticize* when you say what
you think is wrong or bad about
someone or something. *Criticism* is
the noun of *criticize*.

decisive (adj.)
able to make decisions quickly and in a confident way

dominate (v.);
dominant (adj.);
dominance (n.)
1) To *dominate* something is to be the most important or easily seen part or *characteristic* of it. A *dominant* part or *characteristic* is the one that is most important or easily seen.
2) If you *dominate* someone or something, you control or *influence* what they think or do, often in an unpleasant way. *Dominance* is the noun of *dominate*.

dramatic (adj.)
1) exciting and attracting attention
2) connected with acting and the theater.

efficient (adj.);
efficiently (adv.)
Working well and in the best way. *Efficiently* is the adverb of *efficient*. *Inefficient(ly)* is the opposite of *efficient(ly)*.

element (n.)
Fire, air, earth, and water are the four *elements*. In the past, people believed that everything was made from them.

employee (n.)
someone who is paid to work for a company or person

energetic (adj.);
energetically (adv.)
An *energetic* person is enthusiastic and has a lot of energy when doing things. *Energetically* is the adverb of *energetic*.

evaluate (v.)
to decide how good or bad something is after studying or thinking about it carefully

extreme (adj.)
very strong or large in amount; more than most other things or people

extrovert (n.)
A lively, *energetic* person who enjoys being with other people. An *introvert* is the opposite of an *extrovert*.

eyebrow (n.)
An *eyebrow* is the line of hair above each eye. If you raise your *eyebrows* at something, you move your *eyebrows* up to show that you are surprised by it or don't approve of it.

factor (n.)
one of several things that cause or *influence* a situation

feedback (n.)
an opinion about something, often your work, that can help you to improve it

figure (n.)
a picture or drawing in a book or document, usually identified by a number or letter

flexible (adj.);
flexibility (n.)
Able to change easily because this is better for a situation. *Flexibility* is the noun of *flexible*.

focus (v. and n.)
You *focus* on something or someone when you give them a lot of attention or effort, often more than you give to other things or people. Your *focus* is the thing or person that you are *focusing* on.

form (n. and v.)
The *form* of something is the way in which it exists (= is there in the universe). To *form* is to begin to exist or to make something begin to exist.

function (v. and n.)
To *function* is to work or perform. If something is a *function* of other things, its value or *characteristics* depend on the other things and change with them.

idiot (n.)
a stupid person

implementer (n.)
a person who starts using a plan, *system*, etc.

inducement (n.)
something that you give or offer to someone as a reward in order to persuade them to do something

influence (n. and v.)
When something or someone affects what a person thinks or does. A good *influence* makes a person behave well. A bad *influence* makes them behave badly. *Influence* is the verb of *influence*.

inherit (v.);
inheritance (n.)
You *inherit* the same appearance, personality, qualities etc. from your parents or grandparents. Your *inheritance* is the appearance, personality, qualities etc. that you *inherit*.

inspire (v.);
inspiration (n.);
inspirational (adj.)
To *inspire* someone is to make them want to do something and feel that they are able to do it. *Inspiration* is when a thing or person gives you new ideas or makes you want to do or create something. *Inspirational* is the adjective of *inspiration*.

interact (v.)

If two or more people *interact* with each other, they *communicate* with each other, work or spend time together, etc.

introvert (n.);
introverted (adj.)

An *introvert* is a quiet, shy person who prefers to spend time alone. *Introverted* is the adjective of *introvert*. An *extrovert* is the opposite of an *introvert*.

lean (v.)

to move the top part of your body toward or against something

logic (n.);
logical (adj.)

Logic is the way that a person or thing connects ideas when they are explaining something or giving reasons. It is also the name for the science that studies and describes this. If something is *logical*, it connects ideas or reasons in a sensible way.

modest (adj.);
modesty (n.)

If someone is *modest*, they do not like talking about how good, clever, beautiful, etc. they are. *Modesty* is the noun of *modest*.

observe (v.);
observer (n.);
observation (n.)

1) To *observe* something is to see or notice it.

2) To *observe* a person or thing is to watch them carefully, sometimes because you want to learn more about them. An *observer* is a person who attends an event, meeting, class, etc. to listen and watch but does not usually take part in it. *Observations* are the things that you notice when you *observe* something or someone.

optimist (n.);
optimistic (adj.);
optimism (n.)

If you are an *optimist*, or if you are *optimistic*, you see the world positively and expect good things to happen. *Optimism* is seeing the world positively and expecting good things to happen. *Pessimist(ic)* is the opposite of *optimist(ic)*.

passive (adj.);
passivity (n.)

Accepting things that happen and not trying to change anything. *Passivity* is the noun of *passive*.

perceive (v.);
perception (n.);
perceptive (adj.)
How you *perceive* someone or
something, or your *perception* of
them, is the particular way that
you think of or understand them.
A *perceptive* person notices or
understands things, for example
people's feelings, quickly and well.

perfectionist (n.)
a person who wants to do something
as well as possible and is not happy
with anything less than this

performer (n.)
A person who performs, for example
sings, dances, acts, or plays music,
in front of a group of people. In this
text, a *performer* is a person who enjoys doing things in front of people
as part of their job, for example
leading meetings, giving talks, etc.

pessimist (n.);
pessimistic (adj.)
If you are a *pessimist*, or if you are
pessimistic, you see the world negatively
and expect bad things to happen.
Optimist(ic) is the opposite of *pessimist(ic)*.

power (n.);
powerful (adj.)
If you have *power*, you are strong and
able to do things, or can control what
other people do. You are *powerful*.
A *powerful* handshake is strong in a
physical (= using the body) way.

predict (v.);
predictable (adj.);
predictability (n.)
To *predict* something is to say or write
what you think will happen in the
future. If someone or something is
predictable, you know what they will
probably do or what will probably
happen. *Predictability* is the noun of
predictable.

process (n.)
a series of stages or steps taken to
achieve a result

profit (n.)
the money that you make by selling
things or doing business, after you
have paid the costs

realist (n.);
realistic (adj.)
A *realist* sees and accepts what is
really true about a situation and tries
to deal with it in a sensible way. If
something is *realistic*, it is sensible and
possible to achieve.

reality (n.)
the things that really happen or are true, and not the things that you imagine

resourceful (adj.);
resource (n.)
A *resourceful* person is good at finding *solutions* or ways of doing things. A *resource* is something that you can use to help you achieve something.

risk (n. and v.);
risky (adj.)
A *risk* is a chance that something bad might happen. If you take *risks* or if you *risk* doing something, you do something even when something bad might happen because of it. If something is *risky*, it involves *risks*.

routine (n. and adj.)
A *routine* is the things that you usually do each day or week, and how or when you do them. *Routine* work is boring and ordinary.

self-critical (adj.)
A *self-critical* person often *analyzes* their own faults or the things that they don't do well.

sense (n. and v.)
A *sense* of something is a feeling or understanding about it. If something makes *sense*, you can easily understand it. If you make *sense* of something, you understand it even when it is difficult or *complex*. To *sense* something is to feel it and know that it is there.

solution (n.)
a way to solve a problem

stable (adj.);
stability (n.)
A *stable* person is calm and not easily upset. *Stability* is when a situation does not change or is not likely to change.

stubborn (adj.);
stubbornness (n.)
A *stubborn* person does not want to change their ideas or listen to what other people think. *Stubbornness* is the noun of *stubborn*.

submission (n.);
submissive (adj.)
Submission is when you allow someone to control you and accept that you will obey them. A *submissive* person always obeys other people and never disagrees with them, even when they are not kind or right.

surround (v.);
surrounding (adj.)
If you are *surrounded* by things or people, they are all around you. A *surrounding* thing is all around something.

system (n.);
systematic (adj.)
A *system* is a way of organizing or doing things. A *systematic* person or thing does something in a careful and complete way that follows a *system*.

task (n.);
task-focused (adj.)
A *task* is something that you have to do, for example a piece of work. If you are *task-focused*, your *behavior* and activity *focuses* on the task that you have.

theory (n.);
theoretical (adj.)
A *theory* is an idea that tries to explain why something happens or exists (= is there in the universe). If something is *theoretical*, it is based on ideas and not real experience or use.

unique (adj.)
being the only one of something, or good and special in an unusual way

verbal (adj.);
nonverbal (adj.)
Verbal means using words or speech. *Nonverbal* communication, for example *body language*, does not use words or speech.

Penguin Readers

Visit **www.penguinreaders.co.uk**
for FREE Penguin Readers resources
and digital and audio versions of this book.